Black Patriots in the American Revolution

A DANGEROUS SEARCH

Book 1: From Lexington to Bunker Hill

NANCY I. SANDERS

With illustrations by Stan Jaskiel

HistoryCompass

Boston, Massachusetts

HistoryCompass
www.historycompass.com

© 2013 Nancy I. Sanders
1st edition

ISBN 978-1-932663-22-8 paperback edition

10 9 8 7 6 5 4 3 2

Printed in the United States.

Table of Contents

DEDICATION:

This book is dedicated to my husband, Jeff, in celebration of our twenty-fifth wedding anniversary. Your love for history and your natural way of telling stories has inspired me to write stories about America's past. We've had twenty-five wonderful years together, and I'm looking forward to creating new memories with you in the years ahead!

ACKNOWLEDGMENTS:

Some of the research for this project was accomplished with the help of the following key people, whose cheerful assistance and expertise is appreciated far beyond what words can express. Thank you to Anne Bentley from the Massachusetts Historical Society; Martin Blatt, Sheila Cooke-Kayser, and Emily Prigot from the Boston National Historical Park; Susan Halpert from the Houghton Library of the Harvard College Library; and Bea Julian from the DeSable Museum of African American History.

Chapter One

"I hear you got a special letter to deliver to Boston," Tobias said to Isaac Morgan, who was sitting at a table in Buckman Tavern.

Isaac looked up from his bowl of stew. "I'm leaving within the hour. As soon as I get my orders, that is," he said, glancing upwards toward the ceiling.

Tobias knew what Isaac meant. Important men were upstairs in the rented rooms above them. Men had been coming and going for days, stopping at the tavern in Lexington, Massachusetts where 12-year-old Tobias Gardner worked in the kitchen during the spring of 1775.

Some of the men who came to the tavern were Patriots, fiery and hot-headed, speaking loudly in defense of the colonists' rights. They often drew crowds of locals around them, eager to hear their words about the injustices of King George and the dreaded taxes.

Other men stopping at the tavern were Loyalists, or Tories, strong supporters of the British Crown. Tobias knew who they were because these men talked quietly in small groups, trying not to be noticed. It made the hair stand up on the back of Tobias's neck when he carried their meals to them or pocketed a shilling they gave him after running one of their suspicious errands. Tobias always felt like they were watching him, like they were watching everyone and everything that went on at the tavern.

He knew some of them were spies. But Patriot or Loyalist, he didn't care. Politics meant nothing to him.

Tobias shifted the tray of dirty platters he carried, balanced on his shoulder. "I need to get a letter to my uncle in Boston right away," he told Isaac. "Will you deliver it? I can pay."

Isaac shrugged without looking up from his food. "Get it to me afore I leave—that's all I can say. Once I get my orders to ride, I'm gone."

Tobias headed back to the kitchen. He tried to ignore the knot of worry growing in his stomach. He hadn't heard from his uncle since Christmas, when his uncle had sent a letter saying he would come to the tavern the first of April to get Tobias and bring him home to live with him in Boston. The first of April had come and gone without a single word from his uncle. Each day, the knot in Tobias's stomach grew bigger. By now, April 18, the knot felt so big he could hardly eat. What if something had happened? What if his uncle wouldn't come? What if his uncle *couldn't* come?

Lowering the platters into a tub of dirty dishwater, Tobias quickly wiped his hands on his breeches. He just *had* to send a letter with Isaac tonight. He didn't know when a chance like this might come again.

Going back to look at the customers, Tobias narrowed his eyes and scanned the noisy room. Knives and forks clinked. Men's voices rose and fell. He looked at Isaac Morgan, still sitting alone. Empty bowl pushed away from him, Isaac's legs were spread out and his head thrown back. Isaac looked as if he was sound asleep, but Tobias knew it was just an act. The man was alert and ready to jump at a moment's notice. Tobias could tell by the way he held his hand close to the pistol he kept hidden under his coat. But no matter if Isaac was awake or asleep—he wasn't the man Tobias needed. Isaac might be able to deliver a letter, but like Tobias, Isaac couldn't read or write. No. Isaac wouldn't do.

Tobias looked for Nathaniel Wyman, who had read his uncle's letter to him last Christmas. Nathaniel wasn't at the tavern tonight. Tobias made his way around the crowded tables and stopped at a group of five men, farmers in town hoping for a hint of the most recent news.

Tobias interrupted the group. "Anyone here willing to write me a letter tonight?"

After pausing for a brief second to look at him, the men went back to their conversation, not bothering to reply. Tobias knew by their actions that they, like he, had never learned their letters.

Tobias looked out over the room once again. He clenched and unclenched his fists. Probably none of these men could write. They were all rough locals. Farmers and drovers and blacksmiths and such—they had no use for schooling.

But the men upstairs—now that was an idea. They were important. Leaders of the Patriots. They would know their letters. For a moment Tobias thought of climbing the steps and knocking on their door even though he was sure the proprietor, John Buckman, wouldn't like it.

Isaac Morgan interrupted Tobias's thoughts. "Here's my fare," Isaac said, walking past him and thrusting a coin into Tobias's hand. "I'm going outside to stretch my legs."

Tobias followed Isaac through the door and outside into the cool evening air. "Have you seen Nathaniel Wyman around? I need him to write my letter."

Isaac pointed toward the village green. "He can't write your letter tonight. He's out practicing with the other Minutemen."

"But I've got to send my uncle a letter!" Tobias cried, seeing the colonists drilling in front of them. He started to run off toward them, but Isaac grabbed him by the arm.

Isaac spoke through clenched teeth. "Not tonight, I said." He glanced around to make sure no one was listening. Lowering his voice, he said, "Rumors are that His Majesty's troops will soon be on the move."

A window opened behind them, just above their heads. "Morgan?" a man's voice called softly down.

Isaac looked up toward the window and nodded. He let go of Tobias's arm. "There's no time for your letter now," he said. And then he was gone.

The knot in Tobias's stomach doubled in size. Blinking quickly, Tobias took a deep shuddering breath. If he couldn't send a letter to Boston, he'd just have to go there himself and find out why his uncle had never come for him.

The men in front of him marched in two lines, turned as a unit, and practiced aiming their muskets on command. Tobias saw the familiar faces of the local militia who had been gathering more and more frequently here on Lexington Green. A lot of the faces were white—men like Ebenezer Monroe and Caleb Harrington. But some of the faces were black, just like his own. Tobias recognized Prince Easterbrooks and Henry Hill marching within the ranks.

Tobias knew most of the men because they usually came to the tavern after practice. Buckman Tavern was the headquarters of the Minutemen. It was the place to find out the latest news about the brewing unrest in Boston between the American colonists and the British troops.

But Tobias didn't care. He wasn't interested in any news from Boston except from his uncle. Since his ma and twin sisters had died last summer from the smallpox, Tobias didn't care about anything except counting the days until the first of April, when the term of his indenture was over at Buckman Tavern. Then he could go and live in Boston with his Uncle John and Aunt Sarah and three cousins, Abigail, Sadie, and Marie. But the first of April had passed, and he still hadn't heard a word. For all he knew, his uncle might be dead!

With a flutter of wings and a loud caw, a black crow suddenly landed on the top of Tobias's head.

"Davy!" Tobias cried, startled for just a moment. "Where have you been?" He held out his arm and his pet crow hopped off and landed on Tobias's wrist. Davy carefully dropped a shiny brass button on Tobias's outstretched palm.

"I don't care if you brought me a present!" Tobias scolded his crow while he petted the glossy wings with his free hand. "You didn't come home last night. I hardly slept at all from worrying about you!" Just then a clatter of hoof beats sounded behind them. Tobias turned to see Isaac Morgan galloping away in the gathering dusk.

"You can't be flying off and leaving me no more," Tobias whispered to Davy, staring down the road. "You got to stay close. We're running away to Boston the first chance we get."

Chapter Two

"Tobias!" John Buckman called from the door of the tavern. His large hands were plunged deep in the pockets of the apron he always wore.

Tobias whirled to face the proprietor as Davy flew up into the air with a startled caw.

"The militia will be comin' in right soon," Mr. Buckman said. "I'll be needin' you to serve their victuals. Now be movin' smart about it!"

Tobias's heart quickened as he slid past Mr. Buckman's unmoving bulk and through the tavern door. Had Mr. Buckman heard him telling Davy about their plans to run away?

Behind him, he heard Captain John Parker's voice dismiss the men from their drill out on the village green.

"Tobias!" called Fanny, one of the cooks, from the kitchen. "Meat is ready to serve."

James Carnes grabbed Tobias's shirtsleeve. The farmer held up his tankard from where he sat at the table near the huge fireplace dominating the room. "Fill it up again," he said.

"And throw some more wood on the fire," another man ordered. "There's a chill in the air tonight."

For the next few hours, Tobias hurried from one task to the other. The tavern bustled with customers, hungry and cold. Everyone offered loud opinions about the colonist's unsettled state of affairs. Finally, around ten in the evening when Tobias could hardly keep his eyes open a minute longer, the great room was almost empty. Most of the men had gone home.

A large hand clamped down on Tobias's shoulder. "Get yerself some sleep now," John Buckman said in a jovial voice, triumphant with the success of the evening's busy crowd. "You've done yerself a fair night's work, that's for sure." The proprietor boxed him playfully on the head.

Tobias ducked. With an unexpected yawn he couldn't hide, he gratefully headed to bed. Stopping a moment to peer outside the main door, Tobias called softly into the night, "Davy!"

The crow, waiting nearby, flew down and landed on Tobias's shoulder. Together, they walked back into the tavern and into a small room toward the rear. Tobias shut the door behind him. Davy hopped off his shoulder and perched on the back of a wooden chair next to a straw mattress on the floor. With a deep sigh, Tobias settled down on the mattress, pulled a blanket over him, and promptly fell asleep.

Sudden drumbeats pounded. Bells rang. A gunshot exploded nearby.

Tobias bolted up out of bed. His heart pounded in his ears. What was going on? Men's voices now mingled with the ringing of the bells and the beating of the drum. Another gunshot was fired.

"Stay here, Davy!" Tobias instructed, shutting the door behind him. He raced through the tavern and outside to the village green.

"The regulars are out!" was the common cry as men started to gather on the village green. As each member arrived, Captain John Parker organized the Minutemen into formation.

Tobias rubbed his tired eyes. He looked up at the moon, shining brightly over the colonists assembling on the village green. Why, it was only midnight!

John Buckman stood just behind Tobias, barking out orders. "Post a guard upstairs at their door. Get fresh horses for the men. Keep shootin' into the air to alert the neighborhood. Paul Revere said the regulars are out!"

Lights flickered on in the homes surrounding the green. Men on horseback clattered through the crowd. All was confusion, noise, and fear. Tobias caught his breath. Were the British soldiers actually coming tonight? To fight?

Captain Parker seemed to think so. As the Minutemen paced nervously back and forth on the green, muskets and flintlocks glinting in the moonlight, the captain sent riders down the road to report any sightings. None of the riders returned. The road appeared empty from Boston to Lexington. But was it?

Finally, Captain Parker dismissed his men. "Listen for the drums!" he cried. "Return at once when they sound."

With a start, Tobias realized most of the men were heading toward the tavern. He would be needed. He hurried inside, nearly bumping into Mr. Buckman.

"There will be no more sleepin' tonight," Mr. Buckman announced, his earlier jovial mood gone. "Stay alert and be watchin' on the ready."

Tobias nodded. On his way to the kitchen, he stopped at his room and opened the door. Davy flew out and landed on his shoulder. Together, they went into the kitchen.

"Get that crow out of here," Fanny instructed. "I'll not have him in my kitchen tonight. And here," she said, thrusting a bucket of dirty dishwater into Tobias's hands. "Toss this outside."

Davy rode on Tobias's shoulder as he carried the bucket outside and emptied it on the grass. "Stay close, now," Tobias warned as the crow flew to the low branch of a nearby tree. "Remember our plans. And keep out of trouble!"

A sudden tall shape loomed near in the darkness. With a start, Tobias recognized Prince Easterbrooks.

With a start, Tobias recognized Prince Easterbrooks.

"It's a mite cold waiting here outside," Prince said in a deep voice, rubbing his hands briskly together.

Tobias understood what Prince was trying to say. A former slave, Prince had been granted his freedom to enlist as a Minuteman when the Continental Congress called for the organization of localized colonial troops last December. Used to being ordered to stay out of the way, Prince felt more comfortable standing with the servants than sitting in the large room of the tavern where the rest of the Militia were now waiting.

"Fanny will get your plate ready in the kitchen as usual," Tobias said. "It's warm enough in there."

With a grateful nod, Prince headed inside.

For the next few hours, Tobias forgot how tired he was. He was kept busy wiping the tables, filling the tankards, and throwing more logs on the fire. The village bells continued to ring. Occasional gunshots were fired. More and more men responded to the calls of alarm until the tavern was full. Everyone, including Tobias, listened anxiously above all the noise—waiting for one distinct sound.

Finally it came.

Rat-a-tat-tat. The drums beat out loud and clear in the early hours of the dawn.

Tobias almost dropped the heavy tray he was carrying. Men jumped to their feet and grabbed their guns. Several benches tipped over and crashed to the floor. Everyone pushed past each other in their rush to get outside.

The British were marching into Lexington!

Chapter Three

Tobias rushed out the door, bumping headlong into John Buckman. "Stay here, Tobias," the proprietor said, clamping a beefy hand down upon his shoulder. Startled, Tobias stopped in his tracks. What could be needed now?

Mr. Buckman reached for a key hanging from the bunch at his waist and shoved it into Tobias's hand. He jerked his head toward two men hurrying up the tavern staircase. "Unlock their door. And be quick about it!"

Torn with a burning desire to rush to the village green and see the British marching into Lexington, Tobias hesitated.

"Go on, I said!" Mr. Buckman barked. "There will be plenty of time for excitement as soon as you're done."

Tobias turned on his heel and headed to the stairs. Leaping up two and three steps at a time, his heart pounded to the beating of the drum still calling the Minutemen to the village green. The clanging bells filled his ears. Almost out of breath, Tobias reached the second floor of the tavern.

Glancing up, he recognized Paul Revere, a regular customer at the tavern. Paul and another man were waiting at one of the bedroom doors.

"Quickly, now," Paul commanded. "We've no time to waste."

Tobias turned the key in the lock and pushed the door open. The two men rushed over to a window to look at the battle forming below. Tobias joined them.

"See there," Paul pointed. "It's Major Pitcairn!"

Tobias looked at the ranks of British soldiers forming lines on the green below. Major Pitcairn rode his horse back and forth along their side. A stab of fear clutched Tobias's throat. The soldiers looked terrifying in their bright red uniforms with their steel bayonets glinting in the rising sun. And there were so many of them! How could the few colonists, most of them farmers, dare to stand against them?

Paul Revere and his friend had moved away from the window and were busy stuffing papers into a trunk. "Help us, lad," Paul said. "The British must not get hold of Samuel Adams' papers or we'll all be hanged."

Tobias moved quickly, gathering up the various piles of papers that lay about the room. Suddenly a thought struck him.

"Do you live in Boston?" Tobias asked.

"Yes, of course," answered Paul Revere, bending over the trunk and organizing the things inside.

"Do you know of a man named Prince Hall?"

"He owns a tannery shop," Paul answered.

"That's the one. My uncle works in that shop." Tobias added one last pile of papers to the trunk.

Paul Revere snapped the trunk lid closed and straightened. He narrowed his eyes and looked down at Tobias. "There's talk that Prince Hall and his friends were seen visiting the British troops. We have spies everywhere."

"Come on, man," his friend urged. "Let's get this trunk away from here."

Paul Revere and his friend shouldered the trunk together and headed out of the room.

"Where is Hall's shop?" Tobias called out, running after them.

"The Golden Fleece is located on Water Street," Paul answered without looking back. "But if you want to play your politics right, you'll stay away from anyone with Loyalist sentiments." The two men carried their load down the stairs and out the door.

Tobias hung back. He didn't care about politics. He didn't care about anything except finding his uncle. And now he knew where his uncle might be. He had to figure out a way to get to Water Street in Boston!

Suddenly a shot rang out. Then another. And another! Tobias rushed through the door to the battle raging outside.

Chapter Four

Chaos and confusion exploded on the Lexington Green. Right in front of Tobias, the British soldiers rushed into the small group of Minutemen. They charged with bayonets thrusting forward. More shots rang out!

Several colonists fell to the ground. The other Minutemen turned and fled. They were no match for His Majesty's royal troops. Musketballs flew through the air. The people who had been watching ran to the safety of the nearby buildings.

A great fear froze Tobias's feet. He stayed rooted to his spot near the tavern door. Caleb Harrington was down! And Ebenezer Monroe!

The wave of red uniforms and flashing steel drew back away from the green. A sudden cheer went up among the British troops. "Huzzah! Huzzah!" they cried, raising their guns in triumph. Major Pitcairn gathered them together. To the pounding rhythm of the beating drums and the shrill whistle of the fife, they marched off down the road, heading toward Concord. Within a minute, it seemed, they were gone.

Tobias felt sick as he looked at the still figures of the men lying, scattered across the green. It looked as if two dozen colonists had been killed. But wait! Some of the men were moving.

Ebenezer Monroe moaned from where he lay sprawled out on the grass, his musket lying silent beside him. Tobias watched

Prince Easterbrooks hurry across the green to kneel at his side. Suddenly, Tobias's feet had wings. He flew to join Prince at Ebenezer's side. Kneeling next to the wounded man, Tobias choked at the sight of the blood spattered across his face and shoulder.

Ebenezer's eyes fluttered open. He reached up to touch the side of his head. Moaning again, he tried to move.

With trembling hands, Tobias reached inside his pocket for a handkerchief as Prince helped Ebenezer sit up. Tobias gently wiped the blood away from the man's face.

"It knocked me clean out," Ebenezer said. "I ain't hurt too bad."

Other colonists moved back and forth around them to tend to the wounded and carry off the dead.

Captain Parker suddenly shouted, "Gather together, men! They're off to Concord, and so are we."

"After them!" cried a man's voice.

"Yes, let's go!" cried another.

The drummer began to beat his drum.

Prince looked at Tobias. "Stay here till someone comes to help." Prince stood up, tall and straight. "There's more fighting coming, and I'll do my part. We'll make them pay for what they done here today. It's war now, and nothing less."

Tobias looked up at Prince, fear clutching his heart.

"Keep yourself safe, you hear?" Prince said. He turned on his heel and headed toward Captain Parker and the gathering men.

Just then several colonists arrived to help Ebenezer to his feet. Tobias stood and watched as they half-carried the wounded man across the green.

"Tobias!" John Buckman called from the tavern door. He waved a big hand in the air. "Come here, now!"

Tobias ran over to the proprietor.

"After them blasted Redcoats get done at Concord," the large man said, breathing heavily and sweating even in the cool morning air, "they have to turn around and head back to Boston. They'll pass right by here again. Sometime probably around noon. Talk is that we're plannin' to ambush them. Shoot them off, one by one as they're marchin' along."

Mr. Buckman looked around. "Daniel! William! Bring a wagon 'round to the back." He looked at Tobias. "I'm gettin' a supply wagon ready to send along with the men when they come through Lexington and follow the British troops back to Boston. They'll need food, ammunition, and blankets."

Tobias nodded.

"Help Fanny pack the wagon. Hide everything under a load of straw so no thievin' fools get their hands on it. After the wagon leaves for Boston, come find me double quick. It will be a busy day for you at the tavern, that's for sure. I'll need you to help feed the hungry crowds who will be stoppin' in."

As Tobias headed for the kitchen to find Fanny, he thought his heart would burst. A supply wagon heading to Boston! Now was his chance to find his uncle. His thoughts raced. He should gather his things and get Davy. Tobias didn't care if John Buckman needed him later or not. He planned to hide with the supplies under the straw and leave when the wagon drove off. No one would notice he was there. Tobias clenched and unclenched his fists. Today would be the day. He was going to Boston!

Chapter Five

Tobias spent the rest of the morning helping Fanny pack a wagon with supplies. He made trip after trip from the kitchen to the wagon parked behind Buckman Tavern, carrying the food she prepared to send with the militia on their way to Boston. In between the countless trips, Tobias sneaked off to his room and packed his few possessions into a small bag. When nobody was looking, he tucked the bag in the wagon along with the supplies.

Tobias was worried. He hadn't seen Davy all morning. Every time he put another item in the wagon, he called out to his pet. But no fluttering of black wings or loud caw filled the air. What was that bird up to now? He just had to find Davy! How could he leave for Boston without him?

Just after noon, Tobias was carrying a stack of folded blankets down the stairs of the tavern, when sudden cries reached his ears.

"They're back!" a man's voice shouted. Other voices shouted as shots rang out.

Tobias's heart raced. He stumbled down the steps and out the door. Quickly pushing the blankets underneath the pile of straw that covered the supplies on the wagon, he raced around the corner of the tavern, nearly bumping into Prince Easterbrooks.

Prince grabbed Tobias by the arm and pulled him back behind the corner of the tavern. "Stay outta sight," the man's deep voice commanded urgently.

Gulping for air, Prince leaned against the tavern wall and closed his eyes. Tobias noted fresh blood flowing from a gash on the tall Minuteman's shoulder.

Hugging the corner of the wall, Tobias peered around and looked toward the village green. He scanned the road. Where were the organized lines of British soldiers? Where was the beating of the drums? Where was the sound of the fife?

A small group of Redcoats stumbled into sight. One of them carried a torch. Running along the edge of the village green, the soldiers held the torch close to the edge of a small building. It burst into flames. Two more British soldiers ran into view.

Tobias saw Nathan Wallis and Henry Townsend up at a second story window in a building across the way, pointing their muskets down at the soldiers. Henry Townsend fired and one of the British soldiers fell to the ground. Tobias recognized other Minutemen running behind the buildings, flintlocks glittering in the sun, taking position and aiming their guns toward the road.

Still breathing hard, Prince now crouched next to Tobias. "There was fighting up at Concord," he spoke into Tobias's ear. "The British took the North Bridge but we got it back. There must be nearly 400 of our men out there by now, and more coming in."

Tobias clenched his fists as another building burst into flames.

"The Redcoats gotta get back to Boston," Prince continued. "And quick. But our men been hiding along the road, shooting at them all the way back to here."

"They're scared," Tobias said, as more British soldiers stumbled into town. "They're not even marching no more, just running along in little bunches like scared chickens."

Prince nodded. "We're gonna follow them the whole way back to Boston, shooting as many of them as we can."

Prince gripped Tobias's shoulder. Hard. "You stay outta trouble," he said. And then he was gone.

John Buckman appeared next to Tobias, carrying a long musket. The large man was sweating heavily. "We can't let them burn this wagon," Buckman said. "They'll be leavin' Lexington and headin' back to Boston at any minute. This wagon has to follow them and take supplies for our men back to Boston. No tellin' how long our soldiers will be there."

The proprietor shoved the musket into Tobias's hands. "Stay here. You see any of them blasted Redcoats come near with that torch and you shoot them square between the eyes."

Tobias gripped the musket in his hands until his knuckles ached. Leaning his back hard up against the wall of the tavern, he tried not to think about what he'd do if the British soldiers ran his way. Angry shouts and gunshots filled the air from the direction of the road. From his position behind the tavern, however, Tobias couldn't see what was happening. The stinging smell of nearby flames burnt his nose as smoke billowed through the air. Tobias coughed. He scanned the sky, hoping to find Davy. *Oh Davy, where are you?* he silently cried.

Just then John Buckman appeared again. "They're gone," he said, taking the musket away from Tobias.

Jacob Reed walked up, leading two horses. He hitched the horses to the wagon as John Buckman paced back and forth. "Jacob, you be careful now as you follow them soldiers. Stay well behind our men and out of reach of those British guns."

Mr. Buckman turned to Tobias. "Get inside and help Fanny. Some of our men who fought at Concord have stopped at the tavern to eat before they head on to Boston. Fanny needs your help."

The proprietor moved up next to the horses to talk with Jacob. With both men's backs turned toward him, Tobias knew this was his chance. All he had to do was slip in underneath the straw and hide alongside the supplies. He'd be headed to Boston and on his way to find his uncle. This was it!

Tobias's feet stayed rooted to the spot.

Jacob Reed climbed up on the wagon and grabbed the reins. John Buckman reached out a large hand and slapped the nearest horse on the rump. With a cracking of the reins, the wagon lurched and started off.

Hot tears stung Tobias's eyes as he turned on his heel and ran into the tavern. Stumbling blindly down the hall toward his room, his heart felt like it would break. He couldn't do it! He just couldn't go and leave Davy behind. Since his ma and sisters died, Davy was the only family he had left. How could he leave Davy to go and look for an uncle he wasn't even sure was still alive?

Tobias burst open the door to his room and threw himself down on the bed. Great sobs shook his body. How would he ever get to Boston with all this fighting going on? How could he ever leave to go look for his uncle now?

Caw! Caw! With a flutter of wings, Davy flew down and landed on the back of Tobias's head.

"Davy!" Tobias cried, bolting upright. Davy flew off his unsteady perch and then landed back on Tobias's shoulder. "Where have you been all morning?"

With a start, Tobias suddenly realized what must have happened. When he packed his own things this morning, Davy must have followed Tobias into his bedroom. Without seeing him, Tobias shut the door and locked Davy inside. That's why he hadn't been anywhere in sight!

Now it was too late! With a shuddering sigh, Tobias stood up. Davy rode on his shoulder as he headed back outside. He just had to take one last look before he got stuck in the kitchen helping Fanny for the day.

His heart felt heavy as he took one wooden step after another. His chance had come and gone. Now he'd never get to Boston!

But wait! What was this! Jacob Reed and the wagon of supplies were just pulling back into the yard behind the tavern!

With a stampede of hoof beats and braking wheels, Jacob pulled the wagon to a stop.

John Buckman came running out of the tavern. "What's goin' on?" he cried.

"New British troops have arrived from Boston!" Jacob shouted. "There must be a thousand of them! They're gathering on the road, just this side of Lexington. They've met up with the Redcoats we fought this morning!"

"Wait here," Buckman ordered. "I'll send a man to watch them. They've got to leave right soon or they'll never make it back to Boston before nightfall." He pointed a finger at Jacob. "Be ready. I'll send a man out and let you know when it's safe to leave."

John Buckman headed back inside the tavern.

Jacob jumped off the wagon and stood half around the corner of the tavern, looking toward the road.

Tobias's heart took a leap. He had another chance!

"Davy," he whispered sternly to his crow. "You watch where I hide. Then follow along with the wagon when it leaves."

As if understanding his words, Davy flew off Tobias's shoulder and landed in the branches of a nearby tree.

Tobias knew his crow would follow him wherever he went, now that he saw where Tobias was. Taking one last glance at Jacob to make sure he wasn't looking, Tobias hitched himself up the side of the wagon and slid under the straw. The scratchy, musty smell settled all around him. He felt like his heart would burst with excitement.

He was going to Boston!

Chapter Six

Trying not to scratch himself underneath the itchy straw, Tobias lay tense and stiff in his hiding place. *Caw! Caw!* Davy called out to him from his nearby perch.

The church bell's urgent ring still called the colonial militia in from neighboring farms. Men's deep voices from the village green mingled with the busy sounds coming from the nearby tavern.

Tobias waited. He tried not to breathe. He listened. The wagon beneath him jerked back and forth with the impatient stamping of the horses' hooves. Would anyone discover his secret?

After an hour of endless waiting, Tobias heard the faraway tune of a fife and the muted beating of a drum. The sounds moved farther away until they disappeared altogether.

"They're gone!" a loud voice shouted. Tobias sucked in his breath. It sounded as if the man stood right next to the back end of the wagon where Tobias was hiding. A bead of sweat broke out on his forehead. Would they find him?

The wagon jerked down, then up again. He guessed that Jacob Reed had climbed onto the seat of the wagon. Tobias heard the snap of the reins, and the wagon lurched forward. They were off!

Tobias pitched back and forth as the wagon bounced over the rough road. Inching to his left, he wedged himself slightly under several bundles of food so he wouldn't roll around as much. When he was sure they were far enough away from Lexington, Tobias reached out a hand and parted the straw in front of his face until he had a little space to peek through.

From his hiding spot, Tobias could see out along the side of the road. Colonists ran through the nearby fields, carrying muskets. The Minutemen were going in the same direction as Tobias. It seemed everyone was heading to Boston.

Boom! Tobias's heart raced at the loud explosion. Gunshots rang out in answer. The fighting sounded so close!

"They've got cannons!" someone shouted.

"Stay back out of fire!" another voice called out.

The wagon slowed to a stop, then waited, before moving forward again.

Billows of black smoke rose up from burning buildings as they passed through a small town. Tobias watched from his hideout as men and women stumbled among the buildings, carrying the dead in their arms. They passed several women standing with their hands covering their faces, wailing in grief. Bodies of British soldiers, in their bright red coats, lay scattered along the road where they'd been shot and killed.

And so the journey continued the rest of the day. Town after town on the way back to Boston had been trashed and burned by the British soldiers. Dead bodies lined the roadway. Tobias felt sick to his stomach at the sight of it all. After awhile, he covered the straw back over his face. He didn't want to see any more. He listened to the sounds of shooting and shouting that continued along the way. His eyes grew heavy. He'd hardly slept the night before...

With a start, Tobias woke up. It was pitch black. The wagon had stopped.

Scratch! Scratch! Someone was digging through the straw near the front of the wagon. Tobias's eyes strained through the darkness, but he couldn't see a thing. He must have slept for hours!

The noise continued and moved slowly toward his hideout. What if their wagon had been captured by the Redcoats? What if a British soldier were searching through the straw? Tobias had seen the awful effects of the British bayonets earlier in the day. He tensed his muscles as the noise drew closer.

Should he stay still? Or try to run?

Chapter Seven

Tobias lay tense and stiff. His heartbeat pounded in his ears. *Scratch! Scratch!* The digging came closer. He couldn't bear it another minute.

He yelled, bolting upright out of the straw. With a flying leap, Tobias jumped off the edge of the wagon. A strong, stinky smell sprayed across his back. "Hey!" he shouted, landing on his feet and turning to face the wagon.

A black and white striped tail disappeared underneath the straw.

"Skunk!" men shouted. They ran through the dark toward Tobias, then stopped several feet away. A small crowd formed around him, each man clutching a musket in one hand and covering his nose with the other.

Tobias gave a sigh of relief. None of the men wore British uniforms. He was surrounded by Minutemen.

One of the men in the crowd stepped forward, laughing. Soon everyone laughed, including Tobias. He laughed so hard, tears came to his eyes. The tension from today's fear and fighting melted as a welcome relief.

The man held out his hand toward Tobias.

"Peter Salem," the short, muscular man announced.

"Tobias Gardner," Tobias said, shaking his hand.

"I'd say you just ran into a Patriot skunk guarding the supply wagon," Peter said with a grin.

"Or a British skunk stealing American supplies!" someone shouted from the crowd.

Peter clapped Tobias on the back. "Whatever his loyalties are, it was a skunk, no doubt." Peter eyed Tobias up and down as the men in the crowd drifted away. "I just might be able to find you a pair of breeches and a shirt that don't stink like skunk. Your clothes smell so bad, you'll have to burn the ones you're in."

Tobias's eyes smarted from the sharp smell. "I don't want to take your clothes from you."

"Don't worry," Peter assured him. "Let's see what we can find." Peter turned and led Tobias to a nearby campfire flickering brightly in the dark. Several men sat around it, hugging their blankets close in the chill of the night.

"Solomon! George!" Peter said. "You're both close to this lad's size. Do you have an extra shirt? A pair of breeches?"

Both men shook their heads.

A tall shape came closer to the campfire. "I'll ask around," a deep voice announced. Then the tall shape disappeared.

Within minutes, a pair of breeches and a shirt appeared. Tobias changed quickly. The breeches seemed to fit all right, but the shirt was a mite big. He rolled up the sleeves.

Picking up the offensive clothes with a stick, Peter tossed them into the fire. Sparks flew up and disappeared into the night sky.

"What do you say, men?" Peter asked the group huddled close to the warmth. "Think he smells good enough to spend the night?"

"It will keep the Redcoats away from us, that's for sure," one man said.

A blanket was spread on the ground. Tobias settled gratefully down and pulled the warm blanket up around him.

Peter stood in the center, close to the fire. "Tell us, Tobias. What were you doing in that supply wagon?"

"I'm come to Boston to find my uncle," Tobias explained.

"You ain't here to fight?" Peter asked sharply.

"No, I don't care too much for politics," Tobias admitted. "I won't bother you after tonight. In the morning I'm heading out. I'm bound for Water Street in Boston."

Peter shook his head. "You won't be getting into Boston any time soon, I'm afraid."

The men murmured in agreement.

"There's a war going on now," Peter explained. "A British battleship is anchored in the harbor. Its cannons will make sure no colonists enter the city of Boston. The entire British army is holed up in Boston under its protection. Look around, lad," Peter said, gesturing with his hand.

Tobias peered through the darkness. Campfires dotted the fields as far as he could see.

"Militia is coming in from all over the countryside," Peter said. "We're camping here on the outskirts of Boston, just out of reach of the battleship. Boston is under siege."

Tobias drew in a deep breath and gritted his teeth. "I'll get to Boston," he insisted.

Peter shrugged his shoulders. "I told you the facts." He turned away.

Tobias rolled over and turned his back to the campfire. Behind him, he heard Peter Salem talking with another man. Both men were speaking so low, Tobias strained his ears to hear.

"You think he might be a spy?" Peter asked softly.

"Why else would he be hiding out?" a deeper voice answered. Tobias recognized the voice of the man who had gotten him the new clothes.

Both men moved farther away. Tobias could no longer make out their words. He felt worried. Did they actually think he was a spy? What would they do to him? Would they make him go back to Lexington?

Chapter Eight

Tobias woke up as the first rays of sun shone on his face. He blinked his eyes and lay still on the ground for a minute, pulling his blanket close around him against the morning chill. The campfire had died down to a pile of glowing embers during the night. Men busied themselves around it, rolling up blankets, pulling on boots, and cleaning their muskets. Other men called out to each other from the various militia groups dotted across the fields. A horse neighed.

Tobias heard footsteps right behind him. Tobias turned and looked up. He recognized the tall man from the night before who had gotten him new clothes.

"Mornin'," the man said, his deep voice filled with questions.

Peter Salem walked up to stand next to the tall man. "How's our Patriot skunk smell today, John?"

Tobias sat up and rubbed his eyes.

"Are you sure he's a Patriot?" John asked. "He could be a Loyalist for all we know. Sent here to spy out our camp."

Peter looked down at Tobias and sniffed. "Hard to say with the breeze blowing away from us." He grinned and held out a hand to Tobias. Tobias grabbed his hand and pulled himself up.

"I checked around," Peter explained. "Captain Parker's company from Lexington camped next to ours. It's their supply wagon this stowaway was hiding in. Captain Parker said Tobias's story was on the level. Although I must say he was a mite surprised to learn Tobias was sleeping at our campfire."

Tobias nodded. "I'm no spy. I'm not on anyone's side—Patriot or Loyalist. I just want to find my uncle."

Peter shook his head. "Like I said last night, no one is going into Boston."

"Sorry for the accusations," John said. "You just can't be too careful right now. With the war going on and all."

Tobias nodded. "I understand."

"Captain Parker said you should stop by and talk with him this morning," Peter said. "He'll need help fixing meals for all his men. He said you're experienced with kitchen work."

Tobias looked down at his feet. "I'm done with kitchen work," he said. He looked up again. "I'm planning to get into Boston. One way or another."

The two men looked at each other. Peter cleared his throat. "Well, if you get hungry while you're making your plans, Captain Parker will give you a job. And you're always welcome at our campfire."

"Thanks," Tobias mumbled. He didn't even want to think about joining the war. He took a deep breath. It was time to start making plans.

He said good-bye to the men and walked away. Colonists were everywhere, settling into camp. Hammers pounded. Cooking pots steamed with food. It looked to Tobias as if they were planning to keep Boston under siege for quite some time.

Tobias headed back to the supply wagon. He was worried. He hadn't seen Davy since yesterday. Davy had enough sense to follow him in the wagon all the way from Lexington, he was sure of it. Then why hadn't his pet come to him first thing this morning?

"Mornin'" Tobias greeted Jacob Reed as he stood guard over the wagon of supplies.

Jacob started with surprise. "What are you doing here?" he asked.

"Nothing special," Tobias said.

"Looks like none of us is doing anything special this morning," Jacob admitted. "There's no telling how long this siege will last."

"Mind if I sit here a spell?" Tobias asked.

"Make yourself at home," Jacob answered.

Tobias hoisted himself up to the edge of the wagon and sat down. He didn't know how long he sat there, waiting for Davy to appear. The sun climbed higher and higher in the sky. Sweat rolled down the back of his neck. Where was Davy?

Pangs of hunger finally forced him to move on. He grabbed his small bundle from where he'd hidden it underneath the straw. Tobias jumped down off the wagon. It must be noon, he figured as he headed aimlessly back to where Peter, John, and the others sat eating.

"Get yourself a plate," Peter said. "You look half starved."

With a grateful nod, Tobias got a plate of food and sat down next to his new friends. Even though he was hungry, he hardly felt like eating.

Caw! Caw! With a flurry of wings, a crow landed on the ground next to Tobias.

"Davy!" Tobias cried, sudden joy flooding his heart.

Davy dropped a shiny brass button at Tobias's feet.

"Now you have a Loyalist crow!" John exclaimed. "That there's a button from a British uniform. Are you sure you ain't a spy?"

Peter grinned. "First a Patriot skunk and now a Loyalist crow. What will you come up with next?"

Tobias laughed. He felt happy to have Davy back again. He'd been worried a bullet might have gotten him yesterday along the road to Boston.

Now with Davy here, he could start making his plans.

Chapter Nine

Tobias headed straight for Captain Parker's camp. Davy followed close behind. First thing he planned to do was sneak a letter into Boston.

"Prince!" Tobias called out, spying his friend carrying an armload of branches.

Prince set the branches on the ground, next to a crudely shaped wooden frame. "Now just what are you doing here?" he asked. "If you finally decided to join the militia, you can help me today."

"No," Tobias said. "I got more important things to do right now. I'm gonna send a letter to my uncle in Boston. Where's Nathaniel Wyman? He wrote me a letter once before."

Prince turned his back to Tobias and started piling branches over the wooden frame of his hut.

"Where's Nathaniel?" Tobias asked, stamping his foot with impatience.

"Nathaniel's gone," Prince's deep voice mumbled as he continued his work.

"Gone where?" Tobias demanded. "He's one of Captain Parker's Minutemen. He should be here in camp. I need him to write my letter."

Prince kept right on working. "He's gone, I said. Dead. Shot and killed yesterday on Lexington Green. Didn't you see?" Prince turned around to face Tobias. "There's a war going on. There's no more time for letters."

"I'm sorry," Tobias whispered. He stared down at the ground. "Everything happened so fast yesterday. I saw some of the men get shot. I didn't know Nathaniel was one of them..." His voice trailed off. "I just want to find my uncle."

Prince laid his hand on Tobias's shoulder. "I know. But you got to understand things is different now." Prince turned back to building his hut. "There's only one road in and out of Boston, and it's guarded with British sentries."

Tobias's heart felt heavy at the news about Nathaniel. Why did there have to be a war going on?

Tobias sighed. War or no war, he still had to find his uncle. If he couldn't send a letter, he'd just have to try to sneak into Boston himself. Saying goodbye to Prince, Tobias turned and headed toward Boston.

Everywhere he looked, men were busy building temporary shelters. Some put up sturdy tents covered with sailcloth. Others pounded lumber together to make rough-looking buildings. Still others, like Prince, used whatever they could find—branches, dirt, stones, and brush piled together to form little huts to protect themselves from the blazing hot sun and the cool night air.

As Tobias drew closer to Boston, he walked past men building a new kind of structure. Strong walls of dirt, branches, and fences were being built as defenses against British attack.

Davy flew down and landed on the ground. He dropped something at Tobias's feet. Tobias reached down and picked it up. Another brass button from a British Redcoat. Tobias rubbed the button thoughtfully in his hand before shoving it into the pocket of his breeches where he kept the other buttons Davy had brought him. "Why are you bringing me all these buttons, Davy?" Tobias asked. Davy hopped along beside him and then flew off again.

Suddenly, Tobias sucked in his breath. He hadn't realized he'd walked past the last wall of Patriot defense. Up ahead of him he saw men wearing red and white uniforms. British soldiers!

Tobias scrambled to hide behind a large rock near the road. He peeked carefully out. From his vantage point, he studied the area ahead of him. Water was on both sides of the narrow road ahead of him. Ships with elegant white sails floated at anchor. Tobias was certain they were British ships from the flashes of red uniforms he saw upon their decks. On the opposite shore, he saw row upon row of buildings with church steeples rising high among them. Boston!

But wait! A man walked past Tobias's hideout, along the road leading into Boston. He walked up to the British soldiers. Handing one of the guards a paper, the guard read the paper, folded it, and placed it in his pocket. The soldiers stepped back, their silver bayonets glinting in the sun on the end of their guns, and the man walked past them into Boston.

Tobias leaned back against the rock, careful to stay hidden from the soldiers' view. It was possible to get into the city! He saw it with his own eyes!

Just then, a dirty, old farmer stumbled past Tobias along the road toward Boston. With a start, Tobias recognized the man's face. He was one of the men who visited Buckman Tavern with Paul Revere and the others. He was Billy Dawes, a strong Patriot. Then why was he dressed up in filthy rags like some poor colonial farmer? Why was he stumbling along the road as if he were drunk? And why was he walking up to the British soldiers?

Tobias crouched behind the large rock to watch what happened. Billy Dawes walked up with uneven steps and said something to the soldiers. The guards laughed. One of the guards clapped Billy on his shoulder and laughed even harder. Another guard waved him on past the blockade. Tobias watched as Billy stumbled past the sentries along the road and into the city of Boston.

It was a trick, Tobias knew it. Billy disguised himself as a poor drunken colonial farmer, just to get himself past the soldiers and into Boston.

With a start, Tobias knew what he had to do. If the British soldiers were letting people into Boston, they might let him in too. Yes, they had guns. Tobias had seen the effects of their bullets and bayonets yesterday along the road from Lexington. He remembered what they did to Nathaniel Wyman. But maybe, just maybe, they might let him in. He didn't care about politics. He wasn't involved with the war. He wasn't a threat to the British army.

Heart beating fast, Tobias stood up on wobbly legs. He determined to walk straight up to the sentries and ask permission to enter Boston. He took one shaky step, and then another. Would they let him through? What would the Redcoats do?

Chapter Ten

Heart pounding, Tobias took one shaky step after another toward the British guards. With their backs facing him, the soldiers were busy talking to two men who had just walked out of Boston. The guards stepped aside and let the men through. The two men walked past Tobias and continued down the road away from Boston toward the Patriot camps. Just then, the group of guards turned and marched away. A new group of Redcoats took their place.

These new soldiers saw Tobias. One of them lowered his musket, bayonet flashing in the sun, and aimed it at Tobias. A second guard, taller than the rest, stepped forward. "In the name of King George the Third, state your business!" he barked.

Tobias gulped. "I need to get into Boston to find my uncle."

The tall guard narrowed his eyes.

The first guard stepped closer and thrust his gun forward so the point of the bayonet pushed against Tobias's jacket. "You could be a spy," he said.

Tobias stepped backward, fear knotting his stomach.

"We don't let Patriot spies into Boston," the tall guard announced coldly.

Just then the clattering of hoof beats came pounding toward them on the road out of Boston.

Giving one final jab at Tobias with the bayonet, the guards whirled around to face the galloping horse with its rider.

Tobias turned away. He ran. Behind him, shots rang out. Men shouted. A horse neighed. Tobias kept running. He ran so hard back toward the Patriot lines that sharp pains tore through his side. Finally, he reached a small thicket of trees. Tobias ran into the thicket. Exhausted, he hid behind one of the trees. Pressing his back against the sturdy tree trunk, he panted hard, gulping for air.

With a flutter of wings, Davy landed on his shoulder.

Tobias slid down to the ground. Davy hopped onto his lap. Hand shaking, Tobias petted Davy's glossy black feathers.

"What are we going to do, Davy?" Tobias whispered. He closed his eyes and sighed. There was only one thing to do. Look for another way into Boston.

For the next several weeks, Tobias worked hard. Days were spent cooking and washing dishes for the hungry men in Captain Parker's camp. Nights were spent with Peter Salem, sitting around his campfire or sleeping in the small shack Peter, John, and the other men built out of stones and packed dirt.

One evening, sitting around the campfire, Tobias heard a fife playing sweetly nearby. The music came closer and stopped. Tobias looked up to see a strong, husky stranger.

The stranger lowered the fife from his lips. "Evenin'," he said.

"Evenin'," the men around the campfire answered.

Peter Salem stood up and shook the man's hand. "You're welcome to join us tonight. We could do with some entertainment to pass these long hours away. That's right good fife playing, Mr.—"

"Barzillai Lew," the stranger said. "Folks call me Zeal. I'm with the Twenty-seventh Massachusetts Regiment. From Chelmsford." He squatted down next to Tobias, holding his fife in his hand. "Talk's been going through the camps that you men have seen some action."

One evening, sitting around the campfire, Tobias heard
Barzillai Lew playing a fife.

Peter nodded. "We were up at Concord Bridge. And came back through Lexington. The first day of the fighting. Our men saw plenty of action then."

Tobias hardly listened. He wasn't interested in the war. He excused himself and went inside the hut. Lying down on the ground, he pulled his blanket close around him and stared into the darkness. He *had* to get into Boston. He just had to. Wasted days were going by. Suddenly, he heard the lilting tunes of Zeal Lew's fife. He sighed and listened to the melodies. Before he knew it, he was fast asleep.

After that night, every chance he got, Tobias slipped away down the road leading toward Boston. He hid behind the large rock and watched the British Redcoats guarding the road in and out of the city.

Tobias noticed several things as he watched. Important things. He noticed that different groups of soldiers guarded the post at different times of day. Some soldiers were more strict than others. They stood stiffly at attention and hardly let anyone through. Other soldiers didn't seem to care. One group in particular seemed unconcerned with their business. They laughed with each other, told stories, and leaned against nearby fences.

Tobias saw people slip money into the hands of these guards— and many were allowed to pass through. Nearly every day, he saw this same group of guards allow Billy Dawes go through, disguised as a drunken farmer. Tobias was certain Billy carried letters of important Patriot information in and out of Boston. These soldiers didn't seem to care.

It was this group of guards that interested Tobias the most. He was thinking about them one evening as he finished washing the pots and pans after dinner for Captain Parker's troops.

Carrying a load of trash, Tobias headed through the crowded camps. He walked past men standing in line next to one of the necessary houses. He tried to hold his breath as he passed by the makeshift toilet. The stench was terrible in the hot evening air.

Tobias finally reached a pile of trash and dumped his load down among the rest.

Maybe he could wear a disguise and trick those guards into letting him pass through. He grabbed a stick from the ground. Using it to poke among the trash heap, Tobias looked for something to use—anything to wear as a disguise. He pushed aside an old, rotten blanket and uncovered a broken drum. Tobias grabbed the drum and looked it over carefully. All it needed was a new leather drumhead.

Caw! Caw! Davy flew down and landed at his feet. He dropped a brass button on the ground. Tobias set down the drum and picked up the button. He reached in his pocket and pulled out the other buttons Davy had given him. He had ten matching buttons now, all from British uniforms.

Tobias squatted on his heels and thought. There were trash heaps like this all over the camps. Maybe he could look through them and find an actual British soldier's coat. He could clean up the coat, sew on the shiny buttons he had, and disguise himself as one of the king's soldiers! He didn't care which side he pretended to be on, just as long as he could get into Boston and find his uncle.

Tobias stood up. It was dark now, and the light of campfires dotted the fields. He wandered aimlessly among the crowded camps, noting the location of other trash heaps he could explore tomorrow in the morning light.

Suddenly, Tobias stopped in his tracks. There, sitting quietly by himself at a campfire, was a young man. A small jar of ink sat on the ground next to him. In his hand he held a quill pen. On his lap he held a piece of paper. The man was writing something on the paper!

Unexpected excitement made Tobias bold. "Can you write me a letter?" he blurted out. "I'll pay."

The man's pen paused. He looked up and smiled. "Of course I'll write a letter for you," he said kindly. "I don't need your money, though. Come join me here."

Tobias sat down eagerly. His thoughts raced. If he could get his letter written tonight, tomorrow morning he could pay someone to sneak it into Boston. By tomorrow night he would hear back from his uncle. At last his long search would be over!

Chapter Eleven

Tobias introduced himself. "I'm Tobias Gardner from Lexington."

"My name is Lemuel Haynes," the young man said. "It looks like you have a friend," he added, as Davy flew down to join them.

Tobias held out his arm and Davy hopped up to perch on it. "Davy goes everywhere I go," Tobias said. "He followed me clear from Lexington. On the day of the battle."

"You saw the fighting?" Lemuel asked quickly.

Tobias shuddered at the memory. "It was terrible."

"Look here," Lemuel said with a note of excitement in his voice. He held out his piece of paper for Tobias to see. "I'm writing about the Battle of Lexington right now!"

Tobias stared blankly at the black marks of ink on the paper. He shook his head. "I can't read."

"Oh, that's right," Lemuel said. "You asked me to write a letter for you."

"Yes," Tobias said. "I got to get a letter to my uncle in Boston. He was supposed to come to Lexington the first of April and take me to live with him in Boston. But he never showed up. And since my ma and twin sisters died from the smallpox last summer, I don't have anywhere else to go."

"What about your pa?" Lemuel asked quietly.

"I don't know where he is," Tobias admitted. "He was sold down to Georgia when I was three. I don't ever remember seeing him."

"He's a slave, then," Lemuel said.

"Yes. But my ma was free, so my sisters and I were born free, too," Tobias explained.

Lemuel set the quill he'd been holding back in the jar of ink at his side. "I never saw my pa, either," he admitted. "He was straight from Africa. My mother was white, though. She gave me up to neighbor folk when I was just one month old."

"You never knew your ma?" Tobias whispered.

Lemuel sadly shook his head. "Once, when I was about your age, I saw her in town. Folks pointed her out to me and told me who she was. But when I walked up to her, she refused to talk with me. I embarrassed her because of my dark skin."

Tobias sat silent for a moment.

"That's why this war is so important," Lemuel said, picking up his pen again. "That's why the battle at Lexington was so important. It started this war." He pointed to the paper he'd been writing on. "Here, listen to this:

The Nineteenth Day of April last
We ever shall retain
As monumental of the past
Most bloody shocking Scene

Then Tyrants filled with horrid Rage
A fatal Journey went
And unmolested to engage
And slay the innocent

"You wrote that?" Tobias asked.

Lemuel nodded. "Yes. Tyrants like King George in England want to make the American colonists their slaves. And tyrants here in the colonies want to make the Africans their slaves.

Your father shouldn't be a slave. He should be free. My ma shouldn't be ashamed of me just because my pa was from Africa. It shouldn't matter where we're from. We're all living here now. We should all be free and treated equal as equal alike. If it takes this war to bring freedom to our land, it's worth it. Liberty is worth fighting for."

Tobias stared into the glowing flames of the campfire. "I guess I haven't given much thought to the war. I've been so busy trying to find my uncle that all the talk I've heard about liberty and freedom just sounded like empty words. I didn't think it was important."

"It's important, all right," Lemuel said. "It's big. Big enough to think about. Big enough to fight for. Big enough to die for."

For a few moments both sat quietly, side by side.

Suddenly, Lemuel sat up straighter. "I nearly forgot," he admitted. "You asked me to write a letter." He reached in a leather pack and pulled out a fresh piece of paper. "What do you want the letter to say?"

Tobias thought hard. "Dear Uncle," he started. "I am ready to join you in Boston. Please come for me right away. I'm with the militia from Lexington at Captain John Parker's camp. We're just outside of Boston." Tobias watched as Lemuel carefully wrote out the words.

Lemuel looked up. "Do you want to sign your name?" he asked.

"I don't know my letters," Tobias reminded him.

"Then today's a good day to start learning," Lemuel said. "I taught myself to read and write. If I can do it, you can too."

Using a short stick, Lemuel wrote Tobias's name slowly in the dirt on the ground between them. "Now it's your turn. Just trace over each letter the way I did." He handed the stick to Tobias.

Tobias held his breath as he carefully traced over each letter.

"That's a fine job!" Lemuel encouraged. "Now, hold the quill like this and dip it in the ink just like I did." Lemuel showed Tobias how to position the quill in his hand.

His letters looked shaky written below Lemuel's neat handwriting, but Tobias drew in a deep breath of satisfaction when he finished. He had written his very own name!

Tobias stood up, clutching the letter in his hand. "Thank you," he said. "This really means a lot to me."

Lemuel smiled. "You're welcome. Come back any time and I'll show you how to write the rest of your letters."

"You will?" Tobias asked.

"Of course. In the meantime, keep practicing writing your name."

"I will!" Tobias said, waving good-bye. As he walked back toward Salem Poor's camp, he folded the letter carefully and tucked it into his pocket.

Tobias hardly slept that night. Every time he closed his eyes, he saw the letters of his name.

Even before the sun was up, Tobias slipped out of his blanket and ran down the road leading into Boston. He reached the large rock and hid behind it. He planned on hiding here all day until he found someone he could pay to sneak his letter into Boston. Peeking carefully out, he checked to see which guards were on duty. It was hard to see their faces in the early morning light.

Suddenly, a hand grabbed him by the collar and pulled Tobias to his feet.

"What do we have here?" a man demanded in a loud voice. "A spy?"

Tobias's heart pounded with fear.

Chapter Twelve

"No, he's not a spy," a second man said. "I know him. He's from Buckman Tavern."

"Are you sure?" the first man muttered, giving Tobias's collar a shake and then letting him go.

Tobias rubbed the back of his neck. He stared at the two men. Sure enough, he recognized one of them. Ephraim was a Loyalist who used to visit Buckman Tavern in the months before the war. Tobias didn't like Ephraim then, and he was sure he didn't like the man now, either.

"You don't care about politics, do you?" Ephraim asked with a sneer. "You don't care about anything."

"I've got nothing for politics," Tobias admitted. He didn't like Ephraim's voice, though, or the feeling that the two men seemed to be laughing at him.

Ephraim held up a shilling. "You used to like these when you ran errands for me at Buckman Tavern. I wager you still like these now. I need someone to carry a letter into Boston for me today." Ephraim tossed the coin at Tobias's feet. "Are you the one for the job?"

Tobias's heart skipped a beat at this unexpected opportunity. "How will I get past the Redcoats?" he asked.

"Leave that to me," Ephraim said. "They'll let you in and out of Boston today without a problem." Ephraim reached in his pocket and brought out a handful of coins. "Soldiers like shillings, too."

Tobias reached down to pick up the shilling from the ground. As he stood up, he narrowed his eyes. "Why don't you go into Boston yourself?"

"Haven't you heard?" Ephraim asked. "There's an outbreak of smallpox in the city. I'm not going to take any chances."

Smallpox! Tobias caught his breath at the news. He knew the deadly effects of the disease. It had robbed him of his mother and sisters. Still, he pocketed the shilling. He wasn't about to miss this opportunity to find his uncle. He followed Ephraim back to speak to the guards. Ephraim gave Tobias his letter and the soldiers waved Tobias past.

"Hurry back," Ephraim called out to him. "The next group of guards come on duty at noon." He laughed. "They might not be as friendly as these gentlemen."

Tobias didn't care about the guards. Once he found his uncle, Tobias planned to stay with him in Boston.

Walking past the ships anchored in the harbor, Tobias looked at the tall buildings of the city in front of him. He couldn't believe this sudden turn of events. Here he was, walking into Boston. Finally! A wave of fresh excitement washed over him, and Tobias began to run. Surely he would find his uncle today!

Once he reached the city, he followed Ephraim's directions and delivered his letter to the British officer whose name Ephraim had given him. Then he ran through the crowded streets, asking the way to Water Street.

Before long, Tobias stood outside the Golden Fleece on Water Street, the leather shop where his uncle worked. Davy flew down and perched on the shop's sign just above his head.

Glancing up at his pet, Tobias heard voices inside the shop. Men's voices. Taking a deep breath, he pushed open the door and stepped inside.

Chapter Thirteen

The strong smell of tanning leather blew over Tobias as he stepped into the Golden Fleece. Two men turned to look at him. One man was tall and thin, standing at a workbench with leather tools near his side. He wore a white powdered wig, fashionable in Boston at the time. The other man was short and muscular, sitting on a nearby stool. He stood up when Tobias walked in.

The taller man spoke. "May I help you?" he asked with kindness and authority in his voice, placing his hand on a wooden drum sitting on the bench in front of him.

"I'm looking for my uncle," Tobias said quickly. "I was told he worked here with Prince Hall."

The tall man wiped his hands on his leather apron. "I'm Prince Hall," he said, "the owner of the Golden Fleece. Who's your uncle?"

"John Gardner," Tobias said. "I'm his nephew, Tobias Gardner."

Prince nodded his head. "John spoke of you. But why aren't you with his family in New Hampshire? And why are you here in Boston? Has something happened?"

"That's what I'm trying to find out!" Tobias exclaimed. "What's this talk about New Hampshire?"

Prince looked closely at Tobias. "Didn't you get your uncle's message?"

Tobias shook his head no.

"Your uncle works for the Sons of Liberty. It became dangerous for him to stay in Boston. He sent his wife and children to New Hampshire to live with her sister, far away from this city. He had to leave Boston so quickly, he couldn't come tell you himself. He paid a man to deliver a letter to you telling you to meet your aunt in Londonderry. I remember it clearly. It was the last night I ever saw him."

Tobias blinked. "You...never...saw him again? Is my uncle dead?"

"No," Prince said. He turned to the other man. "Have you heard any word about him, George?"

"Nary a word," the man said. He held out his hand to Tobias. "My name's George Middleton. I know your uncle, too."

Tobias shook his hand. "But I don't understand. Why did my uncle have to leave Boston? Why haven't you heard from him?"

Prince and George looked at each other.

"Are you Patriot or Loyalist, lad?" Prince asked.

Tobias hesitated, not quite sure what to say any more. Suddenly he remembered the warning Paul Revere gave to him at Buckman Tavern about Prince Hall visiting British troops. "There's talk that you side with the British," he said quietly.

Prince smiled slightly and shook his head. "No," he said simply.

"Why, them's a pack of lies!" George almost shouted. "What will people think to say next!"

"You haven't answered my question," Prince said. "Are you Patriot or Loyalist?"

Tobias stared at the floor. He remembered the words Lemuel Haynes had spoken to him the night before. Words about freedom and liberty for all people. He looked up at Prince. "I've been so busy looking for my uncle that I haven't given much thought to the war," he admitted.

"Your uncle's a Patriot," George said proudly. "So are we. Go ahead, Prince. Tell him the truth. Tobias isn't one of the king's men. I can tell."

The strong smell of tanning leather blew over Tobias as he stepped into the Golden Fleece.

Prince looked straight at Tobias. "Your uncle is a spy. There's a large network of men and women who spy on the British. They carry important information back to our Patriot leaders. John heard the British were going to march into Lexington and Concord in April. If someone found out what your uncle was doing, he would be hanged. His whole family, too. That's why he sent them north. That's why he left Boston. It was getting too dangerous. Too many Redcoats all through the city. Too many British spies."

"We need to get an army together to fight these British soldiers stationed here in our homes," George said. "Every able-bodied Patriot under siege here in the city should enlist. I'd join."

Prince looked at him. "Would the Continental Congress allow Africans to fight in this army? You know the trouble it's caused in some areas when Blacks volunteered to join their local militia."

"We can organize troops of our own!" George exclaimed, pounding his fist on the workbench. "We got a network of free Africans just like us here in Boston. We all want freedom from King George. We want this war to bring freedom to our brothers from the chains of slavery. We should get together an all-black unit of fightin' men right here, right under the noses of the British. We'd put an end to this siege, startin' right here in Boston. Cato Clark would join us. And Hosea Lamb. Why, there's plenty of men! I could lead 'em." He pointed to the drum on the bench Prince had been working on. "Tobias could be our drummer!"

His fiery speech thrilled Tobias as nothing had before. "Do you really think I could?" he asked.

George put his hand on Tobias's shoulder. "Of course you could."

"I found a drum," Tobias said eagerly. "It's in fine condition. All it needs is a new leather drumhead."

"I can give you one of those," Prince Hall said. "I'm putting a drumhead on this drum right here." He returned to the drum he'd been working on. "Look," he said, showing Tobias how to tighten the leather across the top. He worked carefully on the drum until the leather was tight and secure.

Prince reached beneath his workbench and picked up a soft piece of leather. He handed it to Tobias. "Do you think you can fix that drum you found? This should fit it perfectly."

"How much does it cost?" Tobias asked.

Prince smiled. "I'll supply you with this one for free. If you ever need a new one, you can pay me then. Do you think you can fix your drum?

"I know I can," Tobias said eagerly. Then he stopped. "But what about my uncle? And my cousins?"

Prince leaned both hands on his workbench. "Your aunt and cousins are safe in New Hampshire. You can go live with them and forget about all this fighting."

George spoke up. "For all we know, your uncle could be sneakin' in and out of Boston spyin' on the British. He believes in this war. He believes in freedom. You can stay here in Boston and join the troops I'm goin' to organize."

Prince stared at Tobias. "You have to make the choice, Tobias. Will you run away and hide? Or will you stay and fight?"

Tobias clutched the piece of leather in his hands. "I don't know," he admitted. "I need to think."

"Take your time," Prince encouraged. "Think about it. I'll be here in my shop when you're ready to make an answer."

Tobias said good-bye to the two men and walked out the door. He needed fresh air after the heavy, thick smells inside the leather shop. Davy flew down and landed on his shoulder for a brief minute before fluttering up toward the sky again.

Tobias took a deep breath. He wandered aimlessly through the crowded streets of Boston, lost in thought.

Clank. Clank. Clank. The steady rhythm of clanking chains drew up closer behind him. He heard voices moaning and the crack of a whip. Tobias whirled around. A group of slaves, their feet chained together, were walking toward him down the street.

Heads bowed down, men and women shuffled wearily along. Tobias saw a boy his own age chained up among the rest. Their overseer cracked his whip again and shouted, "Get goin', I said!"

Suddenly, strong hands grabbed Tobias, pinning his arms behind his back. A heavy club hit him on the head, and all went dark.

Chapter Fourteen

"Stand up," a rough voice ordered, pulling Tobias to his feet.

Shaking his head, Tobias struggled to clear the cobwebs from his mind.

Strong hands pinned his arms behind his back and pushed him forward. "I've got another one fer the slave gang!" the man's rough voice called out.

"But I'm not a slave!" Tobias cried, twisting and turning to escape the large man's grasp. "I'm freeborn!"

"Be quiet or I'll give yer another blow," he commanded, jerking Tobias along the street.

Caw! Caw! Caw! Davy dive-bombed down from the sky, pecking at the top of the man's head.

"Hey!" the man shouted, gripping Tobias tighter with one hand and swinging at Davy with his club.

Just then the clatter of hoofbeats pounded up behind them. A shot rang out. "Unhand the lad!" cried George Middleton's voice from behind them.

The man kept his hold on Tobias and turned to face the man atop his horse. "My slave's tryin' to run off," he lied.

"That's not your slave and you know it," George said. "You let him go or this time I won't fire my shot up into the air." He aimed a pistol down at the man.

Davy flew in and pecked at the top of the man's head.

The man shouted, swinging his club wildly again.

"Aw, leave him be!" cried the overseer at the front of the gang of slaves. "Let's get movin' on!" He cracked his whip over the men and women in chains, and they slowly walked away down the street.

Scowling, the man shoved Tobias to the ground, turned, and followed behind the slaves.

Tobias struggled to stand up.

George kept his pistol aimed at the man until the gang of slaves disappeared around the corner.

"You all right?" he asked grimly, putting his pistol away. His horse pranced impatiently on the street as George held tightly to its reins.

Tobias nodded. "A little shook up. Thanks, though. Thanks a lot."

George reached down a hand and helped pull Tobias up behind him on his horse. "I thought I should keep an eye out for you today," George said. "Boston's a dangerous place. Slave drivers, Redcoats, hungry citizens, and smallpox. It don't get much worse. Not a good place for a lad like you to be wandering about." They turned and rode the horse down the street.

Just then Davy flew down and perched on Tobias's shoulder.

"That's quite a friend you have there," George said. "By the way, how did you get into Boston today? I thought no one was allowed in or out of the city because of the siege."

"One of the king's men paid the guards. They let me through to deliver a message for him."

"Did he pay you, too?" George asked quietly.

Tobias hesitated. He felt the disapproval in George's voice. "Yes," he admitted. "I have to return by noon."

George glanced up at the sky. "It's almost noon now." They rode in silence for several moments, the clip clop of the horse's hooves making a steady rhythm beneath them.

Tobias felt bad. Had it been wrong for him to help the British? It didn't really matter. Or did it? He shifted uncomfortably behind George, staring at the man's broad, muscular back.

"Whoa," George said, pulling on the reins. Davy flew up and away into the sky. They had reached the edge of the city. The road leading out of Boston stretched before them. British war ships patrolled the waters nearby in the harbor.

George helped Tobias down to the ground. "If you decide to fight for freedom, you're welcome to join my company as drummer, just like I said." He looked Tobias squarely in the eyes. "But I'll not have a traitor in my camp."

As Tobias walked past the guards and headed toward the Patriot camps, he thought about George's words. Traitor. It smarted just to think of the accusation. He remembered everything that had happened today. George Middleton and Prince Hall had talked about the importance of fighting for freedom, just as Lemuel Haynes had.

Suddenly, a series of musket shots rang out in a thicket in front of Tobias. His heart raced. He heard men cheering. What was going on?

Tobias sneaked up and hid behind a tree. Peeking out, he recognized Zeal Lew in front of a crowd of colonists, playing a lively tune on his fife. He was standing next to Peter Salem as everyone cheered. The clearing was crowded with men. On one side of the clearing, Tobias noticed a stack of hay set up as some sort of target.

Relieved to see his friends, Tobias stepped out from behind the tree.

Zeal spotted Tobias and lowered the fife from his lips. "You're looking at the best marksman in Massachusetts," Zeal bragged to Tobias.

Tobias walked up to his friends.

"The men organized a shooting contest," Zeal explained.

Someone shouted out from the crowd, "There ain't nothing

*At target practice, Peter Salem hit the bull's eye every time
and won the shooting contest.*

else to do while we're waiting for the British to make the next move."

Zeal laughed and clapped Peter on the back. "The British better be careful! This man here has hit the bull's eye every time. No one else even came close."

Peter smiled and held up his musket. "I pretended I was aiming at a Redcoat each shot I took."

Suddenly a man shouted from the crowd behind them. "Tobias! What are you doing here?"

Tobias whirled around in surprise. "Uncle John!" he cried.

Chapter Fifteen

"Uncle John!" Tobias cried, running through the crowd. The men parted to let him pass.

Uncle John wrapped Tobias in a big bear hug, then held him out at arm's length.

Tobias didn't know whether to laugh or cry—he felt so happy, so excited, and so relieved all at once.

"Just look at you," Uncle John said, both hands on Tobias's shoulders. "I think you've grown a foot since I last saw you. But what are you doing here? Why aren't you with your cousins?"

In a rush, Tobias told Uncle John everything—about never getting his letter, being in the middle of the Battle of Lexington, helping out during the Siege of Boston, and meeting Prince Hall.

Just as he was finishing, Peter Salem and Zeal Lew walked up. Shaking Uncle John's hand, Zeal said, "Tobias is a hard worker. You can be very proud of him."

Uncle John nodded. "I am. I'm counting on him being a big help to his Aunt Sarah while I'm gone."

"But Aunt Sarah's up in New Hampshire!" Tobias protested.

Uncle John looked surprised. "Isn't that what you want to do? Go stay with Aunt Sarah and your cousins until this war is over?"

Suddenly, for the very first time since the war began, Tobias knew what he wanted to do. The feeling burned like a strong flame within him. "I want to stay here with the other men," he explained. "I want to do what I can in the fight for freedom."

"I don't know," Uncle John said, shaking his head. "War is no place for a boy."

Just then Peter spoke up. "I think what Tobias is trying to say is that he's no longer just a boy."

"Oh—and I almost forgot!" Tobias said, reaching inside his coat and pulling out a piece of leather. "Prince Hall gave me this leather for a drumhead. George Middleton said I could be his drummer."

"Drummer?" Uncle John asked. "Why does Middleton need a drummer?"

"He's forming a unit to protect Boston from the Redcoats," Tobias explained. "He told me I could join his troops as their drummer."

Zeal reached out and fingered the leather Tobias held in his hand. "I'll show you how to put that on a drum. I'll teach you how to play. You'll make a fine drummer."

Uncle John stood for a moment deep in thought. "You know the type of work I'm doing, don't you?"

Tobias nodded. "Prince Hall told me. I haven't told anyone else, though."

"I keep an eye on the British while they're holed up in Boston," Uncle John said, looking at Peter, Zeal, and Tobias. "I report their plans to the Patriot leaders." He took a deep breath. "The British are making plans. Important plans. They're planning how to break out of this siege. It's my job to find out what their plan is and when they will do it. Their next move will be sudden. Dangerous. A lot of men will be killed on both sides. I'd feel a lot better knowing Tobias was safe up in New Hampshire—away from all the fighting."

Tobias stared at Uncle John, the fire of liberty burning deep inside his heart. This fire gave him the courage to speak. "Uncle John, I want freedom from King George as much as you do. I want freedom for everyone, even my father. I believe in this war and I'm willing to die for it."

Uncle John nodded slowly. "You have grown up, haven't you? All right, then." He reached out to shake Tobias's hand. "Keep your whereabouts posted with George Middleton. I'll check in with him now and then to make sure you're all right. He'll let you know how I'm doing as well."

Uncle John shook Zeal's hand. "Tell the men to get ready. It won't be long now. I'll be back as soon as I hear news of the Redcoats' next move." Uncle John reached out and gripped Tobias's arm. Then he turned and headed off into the woods.

For the next couple of weeks, Tobias was busy. He did his usual cooking chores for Captain John Parker and his men. After his work was done, he spent the rest of his days with Zeal, fixing his drum. When it was finally ready to go, Zeal handed Tobias a pair of drumsticks and taught him how to play a steady beat.

One afternoon Tobias was sitting with Peter, Zeal, and the other men around their campfire. Davy hopped about the circle, pecking at scraps the men tossed to him on the ground. They had just finished eating the midday meal. Tobias used a stick to scratch his name in the dirt. He could write his name fairly well by now. He knew his other letters, too. Lemuel Haynes had taught them to him each time he stopped by Lemuel's campfire for a visit.

Tobias dropped the stick and stood up. He wanted to get his drum and practice the new drum roll Zeal had showed him that day.

Just then, a man walked quickly toward him. "Uncle John!" Tobias cried in surprise.

Uncle John came close to the campfire and stood in the center of the men. "It's time," he said. "The British are planning to break out of Boston and take over Bunker Hill." Uncle John looked around at Tobias and the other men. "We have to move tonight. Our men must establish a position on Bunker Hill before the British have a chance." Uncle John turned on his heel, and headed off. "Spread the news!" he called back. "We move tonight!"

Chapter Sixteen

The afternoon flew by in a whirlwind of activity. In every militia company camped across the fields, men busied themselves molding musket balls and cleaning their guns.

Tobias tied a length of string carefully around one of Davy's legs. He tethered Davy to the low branch of a nearby tree so he wouldn't fly off and disappear in all the excitement. For some reason, he wanted Davy to be near him while he practiced beating the drum.

Caw! Caw! Caw! Davy flapped his wings and hopped up and down on the branch, pecking at the string. He was impatient in his eagerness to be free.

"What am I going to do with you tonight?" Tobias asked, holding his drum sticks still for a moment. "I can't let you follow me when we sneak over to Bunker Hill. What if the Redcoats hear you? It would ruin everything."

Tobias walked over to his crow and reached out to pet Davy's glossy black feathers. "I can't leave you tied up like this, though. What if something happens to me and I don't come back..."

Tobias swallowed hard. The realization of what he was doing made his mouth dry. He had seen what the Redcoats did with their guns on Lexington Green. On his wagon ride along the road to Boston, he had seen how they used their bayonets.

Just then Peter Salem walked up. He was holding his musket. It was longer than he was tall. "How's our Patriot Skunk today?"

Tobias took a deep breath and tried to smile.

Peter looked serious. "You don't have to come with the men, you know. There's still time for you to change your mind."

Tobias shook his head. "No. This battle is important. Freedom is important. I'm not staying behind. The problem is I don't know what to do with Davy."

Peter looked at the crow, still pecking at the string. He stood for a moment, deep in thought. "We can't have him following us, that's for sure." Suddenly Peter brightened. "It won't hurt him to stay here for one day. I'll let the other men know where he is. Tomorrow, we'll come back to let him go. Someone will untie him. I promise."

Tobias still felt unsure.

"We're all going up to headquarters at Cambridge for an evening service. There will be preaching before we march out. It will do you good to join us."

Tobias nodded. He petted Davy once last time. Adjusting the shoulder strap his drum hung from, he turned and walked off across the field with Peter. He didn't look back.

Chapter Seventeen

Tobias stood with Peter and the other men in the gathering dusk. They had come to Cambridge, the headquarters of the militia who had been camping outside of Boston during the siege. A short distance through the crowd, Tobias spotted his friend, Zeal, lined up with his company. Zeal caught his eye. Raising the fife to his lips, he played out a merry tune. Tobias smiled as he recognized the notes of *Yankee Doodle*, everyone's favorite song.

Just after sunset, a man walked out in front of the troops. Tobias took off his hat, along with the other soldiers, as the man began to preach. His words brought comfort and somehow helped ease the turmoil of emotions that raged within him. When he finished, a tall, thin man walked out in front of the troops. Even though he was dressed like a farmer in brown homespun, he wore a sword at his side and carried an air of authority.

Peter leaned over and whispered in Tobias's ear. "That's Colonel William Prescott. He's one of the officers in charge."

Colonel Prescott spoke quietly, but Tobias heard his words clearly on that warm June night. "We march steadily toward Charlestown Neck and out onto Bunker Hill," he commanded. "Hold your lanterns low. Cover the light as much as possible. And above all, maintain complete silence. We'll soon be within range of the warships in the harbor."

Without speaking a word, the men turned and headed northeast toward Charlestown, a steady and silent stream of various groups of militia. Tobias fell into step alongside Peter. The night pressed close in around them. With only a sliver of a moon in the sky, it was very dark, except for the eerie glow of lantern lights swinging back and forth across the path. It was hard to see the ground in front of him. Tobias concentrated so he wouldn't stumble or fall. He clutched his drumsticks tightly in one hand. His drum, hanging on a strap from his shoulders, swayed heavily with each step he took.

Suddenly the line of marching men halted. Tobias stopped. They must be getting close—but to what? He wasn't sure. His chest felt tight. He heard the men murmuring in front of him while they waited. He heard questions, passed along the line. No one seemed quite sure what was supposed to happen next.

Just then a group of horse-drawn wagons drove up and stopped at the side of the line.

"Shovels and picks," Peter said in a low voice. "We're to build fortifications, no doubt."

Tobias strained his eyes to see through the darkness. He saw that the wagons were piled high with shovels and other tools for building.

Caw! Caw! A flurry of black feathers dive-bombed from the night sky and landed on the ground next to him.

"Davy!" Tobias said with a groan. "How did you get here?"

Davy hopped on the ground toward Tobias, a short string hanging from his leg.

"He pecked clean through that string," Peter said softly.

Tobias held out his arm, and Davy hopped up to perch on his wrist. "Oh, Davy," he whispered. "Why did you have to follow me here? Now everything is ruined." He turned to look up at Peter. "What am I going to do?"

Peter shook his head. "I'm not sure."

Tobias untied the piece of string, trying to think. When he was done, Davy hopped up to perch on his shoulder.

"We passed some buildings not too far back," Tobias said quickly. "I could double back, put Davy inside a room in one of the buildings, then come join you."

Peter nodded. "It just might work. We haven't moved for a short while. We might not march for a short while longer."

Without wasting another minute, Tobias turned and headed back the way they had just come. Davy rode on his shoulder as he walked back, alongside the line of waiting troops. He hurried as fast as he could. After about ten minutes, he was breathing hard from the strain and the worry. Oh, why did Davy have to follow him here?

Just then the line of men began to move again. With a startled *Caw*, Davy flapped his wings and flew up into the night sky. Tobias stopped in his tracks. "Davy!" he whispered hoarsly. "Come back!" It was no use. Davy had disappeared high in the darkness of the night sky.

Tobias's heart beat fast. Now Davy would follow him for sure. And the troops were marching on to Bunker Hill!

One of the men marching past suddenly stopped next to him and spoke up quietly. "Need help, son?" he asked.

Chapter Eighteen

Tobias stood, his feet frozen to the ground. How could he tell this stranger about Davy? They were supposed to march in silence!

Tobias started to speak, but the man held up his hand.

"Come along, son," the man urged in a low voice. He joined the line of marching militia again.

Tobias hesitated, but the man beckoned to him. Clutching his drum sticks, he hurried forward and joined the man at his side.

They marched silently through the darkness for some time. At some point along the way, the man quietly informed Tobias that his name was Salem Poor.

Walking next to Salem, Tobias felt as if his heart would burst with worry. What should he do about Davy? What if Davy started making noise and alerted the British to their secret activity? What if...?

Suddenly the line of marchers halted once again. Tobias saw Salem peer into the darkness, scanning the area around them. Men along the line began murmuring their questions once again.

Salem held up his hand and the murmuring stopped. "Rest while you can," he commanded in a low voice. His instructions were passed along the line, and the men settled down to sit on the ground. The lanterns were covered so no light escaped.

Tobias sat beside Salem in the dark, letting his drum rest on the ground next to him.

"Tell me now, son," Salem said softly.

Keeping his voice low, Tobias told him all about Davy. After he finished, Salem looked thoughtful for a moment.

"See ahead, there," Salem said, pointing away into the distance.

Tobias strained his eyes to see through the darkness. The salty air of the sea blew gently over him.

"That's the *Lively*. Close by in the harbor. She's a small warship, but dangerous." He pointed again. "There's another British warship. And another."

Just then the *Lively's* bell began to ring. Tobias stiffened in sudden fear, holding his breath. The bells on the other ships rang out. Their sound carried clearly through the darkness. "All's well," came the faint cry from British sentries in response. The bells were silent once again.

Salem looked over at Tobias. "You can stop worrying. The British won't be thinking to notice one small crow. They're ready for war."

Tobias let out his breath. Maybe Salem was right. Maybe Davy would be alright after all.

"I should get back to my friends," he whispered. "They're up ahead."

Salem nodded. "In time. Wait till we move."

After a couple of hours of waiting, orders finally came down the line. Plans for fortifications were mapped out at various points on Bunker Hill. Soldiers were sent quietly to get the shovels, picks, and entrenching equipment from the wagons. It was time to build.

Tobias took his turn with the shovel, building up the dirt walls of the fort. He worked beside Peter and his friends, who were swinging a pick to break up the rock-hard ground. Salem and the men from his militia company worked nearby.

It was hard, frenzied work. Tobias sweated in the warm night air. Every half hour, the bells rang out on the warships guarding the harbor. The voices of the British sentries floated faintly to him from over the water. It was a constant reminder to Tobias of how close the colonists were to danger. The men worked hard and fast, silently through the night, only taking occasional breaks to take turns standing guard.

When the first rays of dawn stretched across the sky, Tobias stopped for a moment and leaned on his shovel. He felt tired and hungry. His shoulders ached. His hands smarted with blisters. Some of the blisters were bleeding.

He looked around. A long dirt wall stretched across the hillside—a strong fortification with troops of militia protected behind. Off to the side, a short distance from the redoubt, or fort, the buildings of the small community of Charlestown were silent. They had been abandoned ever since the siege began. British warships lay sleeping in the harbor. Across the water, the rooftops of the slumbering city of Boston glistened in the rising sun.

He saw Salem standing behind the wall a short distance away, beckoning to him. Tobias hurried over.

"Here's your drum, son," Salem said in a low voice.

Kaboom!

"Get down!" Salem shouted. All the men ducked.

Kaboom! Kaboom!

Tobias crouched down behind the dirt wall next to Salem. Other men pressed in closely. Cannonballs thudded into the hillside. The *Lively* had seen them. The battle had begun!

Chapter Nineteen

Kaboom! Kaboom!

The cannons continued to thunder. The ground shook underneath Tobias as each cannonball thudded into the hillside. He pressed close into the dirt wall for protection, his heartbeat pounding in his ears. The drumsticks poked against his chest from where he carried them tucked inside his jacket. Salem and the other men crowded in close around him. Tobias smelled the sweat from the men's night of hard work. He heard the heavy breathing from their fear.

After half an hour of constant noise and confusion, unexpected silence filled the air.

"Stay low," Salem cautioned the men.

Tobias drew in a long, shaky breath. He couldn't help it. He just had to look. Slowly rising up, he peered over the top of the dirt wall. The sleepy scene he had witnessed just a short time ago was now a busy beehive of activity.

The various warships in the harbor moved through the water as if with a single purpose. British soldiers in their bright red coats collected in large numbers on the shores of Boston. Masses of people gathered on the rooftops to watch.

Tobias noted that there was activity among the American troops as well. Groups of militia hurried away off to the side of Bunker Hill to build new lines of defense. High up in the sky above them, he saw a crow. His heart felt a sudden stab. Could it be Davy?

Salem joined Tobias at his post. "England has the most powerful military in the world," he said grimly.

Tobias swallowed hard. How could they ever hope to stand up against such organization? Such numbers? Such guns?

As if reading his thoughts, Salem said, "We're low on powder. We'll have to keep our wits about us." He looked up and down the wall. "We need to keep working. They'll be coming. Soon." Salem left and spread the word to the other men.

Tobias set down his drum. He grabbed a shovel with new energy, working alongside the men to build the wall even stronger. From a short distance behind him, he heard the merry tune of a fife. The sound grew closer and stopped. Turning around, Tobias felt glad to see Zeal.

Salem came up to join them. "You've done your share of the digging," he said to Tobias. "Now we need a drummer."

"He's right," Zeal said, lowering the fife from his lips.

"These men haven't fought before," Salem explained. "They need courage."

"There's nothing like a fife and drum to keep their spirits up," Zeal agreed.

"Alright," Tobias said, nodding. He handed Salem his shovel and picked up his drum, adjusting the strap over his shoulder. He pulled out his drumsticks.

Zeal raised the fife to his lips and played *Yankee Doodle*. Tobias beat the drum.

Sudden thunder split the air as all the warships in the harbor opened fire.

Boom! Boom! Kaboom! Boom! Boom!

Tobias fell back against the wall. Dirt flew as cannonballs thudded into the hillside.

"Stay down!" Salem shouted. "But keep playing!"

Trying to ignore his wildly beating heart, Tobias played on. Holding his drumsticks with shaky hands, and hugging close to the wall, he beat out the rhythm Zeal had taught him. Zeal played the fife next to him. Both of them kept their heads low.

The roar of the cannons went on and on. It lasted for hours. Tobias's ears rang with the thundering noise. The sun beat down hot and stifling over the men. Their courage weakened with the constant blast from the warships in the harbor. Many of the men began to drift away from the fort. They headed back toward the safety of the Patriot lines, out of reach of the deadly cannonfire, leaving Bunker Hill behind.

Tobias and Zeal played as much as they had strength to, moving among the men as close along the dirt wall as they could. For awhile, they stood near Peter, whose steady work with a pick loosened up more dirt for others to shovel.

Salem Poor seemed to be everywhere, strengthening weak parts of the wall with more dirt, shouting encouraging words to the other men working to build up the wall, and calling back those who started to leave. Cannonballs flew through the air. *Boom! Boom! Kaboom!*

With all that cannonfire, Tobias felt amazed that only one man had been hit. Tobias, Zeal, and the rest of the men were careful to stay down low behind the protection of the dirt wall. At one point, Colonel Prescott climbed up and walked along the wall in the middle of the explosions, shouting words of encouragement to the troops. It was a daring thing to do, but it helped Tobias and the others hold their position at the fort.

By mid-afternoon, Tobias felt weak and thirsty. So thirsty... The hot sun made him dizzy and faint. Still he played.

Suddenly, the cannons stopped. Tobias stopped beating his drum. He leaned back next to Zeal against the dirt wall. His hands felt numb. His drumsticks were bloody from the raw blisters on his hands. He closed his eyes. His ears kept ringing in the silence.

Tobias felt a hand on his shoulder. He opened his eyes and looked into Salem's concerned face. A wave of dizziness swept over him, and Tobias swayed.

Salem held Tobias in his firm grip, and then offered him his canteen. Tobias took the canteen, gulped down a drink, and felt renewed strength.

"Better?" Zeal asked.

Tobias nodded.

Putting the cap back on his canteen, Salem motioned for Tobias and Zeal to look over the wall.

Still hugging the wall close, Tobias glanced over the top. Thirty or forty barges, filled with British troops, floated across the water from Boston, toward their fort on Bunker Hill.

"Here they come," Salem said.

Chapter Twenty

The men in the fort stood quietly, nerves raw, watching the activity down below their position on the hill. The British barges pulled close to shore, soldiers in bright red coats scrambled onto the beach, then the barges set out across the water again to bring more men.

Tobias stood next to Salem, watching the Redcoats who had landed. They formed into organized lines.

More British troops came ashore and set up various positions across the fields.

Suddenly Salem pointed off toward the small community of Charlestown. "They've set it on fire!" he exclaimed as smoke billowed up into the air.

The soldier next to Salem pointed his musket and aimed.

"Hold your shot!" Salem instructed. "Wait till they're close."

The man lowered his musket.

All along the wall of the fort, men stood two and three deep, muskets held ready.

"Don't waste your powder!" Salem called out.

Colonel Prescott came near them, walking along the top of the wall. "Don't shoot till they're close enough to hit!" he ordered.

The British troops started to advance up the hill. Closer and closer they came. The sun beat down on them. Tobias could hardly breathe.

Several men aimed their muskets over the top of the wall.

"Steady," Salem said, holding up his hand. "Not yet."

The troops came closer. Bayonets gleamed in the sun. Closer. Closer. Tobias held his breath.

"Fire!" Colonel Prescott shouted.

Everything exploded around Tobias as the men fired their muskets. The line of Redcoats fell backward from the force of the blast. Those who were still standing turned and ran back to a safe distance away.

Tobias let out his breath. He heard more firing coming from where other American soldiers were stationed throughout the fields. *Kaboom!* Ships were firing their cannons again.

The British troops regrouped below with new men forming the ranks. Most of the first group lay dead or dying on the ground. The Redcoats advanced again.

Salem held up his hand. "Hold your fire," he urged the men. "Don't waste a single shot."

Closer and closer the soldiers came. When they reached the same spot as before, another blast of explosion resounded all around Tobias from the muskets along the fort wall. Again, the line of British fell backwards from the force. The few still standing ran back down the hill. Dead bodies in bright red coats covered the ground.

"Tobias," Salem said, whispering hoarsely into his ear.

"Yes?"

"Do you know how to beat out a retreat on that drum?"

"Of course," Tobias answered. "But why?"

Salem looked up and down the line of men standing behind the protection of the wall. A great number of them had stepped back from the wall and were walking away.

He leaned close and whispered in Tobias's ear again, "Most of the men are out of powder. I have just one shot left. If the British advance again, we'll have to retreat."

He stood up and looked squarely at Tobias. "Get away from the wall, son. Watch for the orders. Then beat out a lively tune and make haste to get back to safety." With that, Salem turned on his heel.

As Colonel Prescott and other officers shouted orders, Salem moved among the men. "Stay and fight!" he urged the soldiers who were preparing to leave. "Defend our liberties!"

Tobias moved away from the wall and stationed himself where he could keep an eye on Salem.

Sudden shouts took most of the men back to the wall. "Here they come!" someone cried. Another explosion of muskets rang out, sputtered, and then stopped.

Chaos and confusion broke out as Redcoats stormed over the wall and into the fort.

Tobias stepped backwards in fear. A British officer climbed over the wall and stood victorious at the top.

Suddenly, the officer fell. He was shot! Tobias saw Peter lower his gun.

The red tide of British troops poured into the fort.

"Retreat!" ordered Colonel Prescott.

Tobias froze.

As if in a dream, he watched Salem Poor from where he had backed away from the wall. Salem carefully aimed his musket toward the top. With a great blast, he fired his last shot. Another British officer fell dead to the ground.

Salem looked over at Tobias. "Retreat!" he shouted. Then turning his musket around, he faced the crowd of British soldiers. Swinging back and forth with the heavy end of his gun, Salem used it to fight in hand-to-hand combat against those deadly bayonets.

"Retreat!" Salem shouted to Tobias one more time, not turning around.

His words finally broke Tobias out of his frozen fear. Tobias beat out the rhythm on his drum. Musketballs flying all around

him, cannon balls thudding to the ground, he hurried with
the other soldiers backwards out of the fort, beating his drum all
the way.

Chapter Twenty-One

It took two full days after the fighting for the swelling to go down in Tobias's hands. Peter had helped wrap strips of cloth around each one to allow the blisters to heal.

Tonight Tobias sat around the glowing embers of the campfire with Peter and the other men, just as he had often done before the Battle of Bunker Hill. The night was warm. The stars shone like diamonds overhead.

Tobias heard footsteps coming toward them through the darkness.

"Salem!" he exclaimed, with relieved surprise. "I wasn't sure you made it out of the fort."

Salem sat down and joined the circle of men. "By the mercies of God, each one of us here survived."

Peter nodded. "It was by God's great mercy alone that so few of our men are gone. The British suffered terrible losses, even though they took over the fort."

"We ran out of powder," Salem said. "Their barrels were still full."

Tobias reached to his side and held up his drum. "A musketball tore a hole clean through the drumhead."

Salem placed his hand on Tobias's shoulder. "I'm glad you're safe, son."

Tobias blinked back sudden tears at the warmth in the man's voice. "Davy—" he began.

"Your crow?" Salem asked.

Tobias nodded. He found his voice. "Davy hasn't been back since." He paused, then whispered. "I think he might have been hit."

"Can you be sure?" Salem asked, looking around the circle of men.

Peter just shook his head.

"I think I saw him flying over the fort before the shooting began," Tobias said. "He's never been gone like this. If he was all right, he would have come back here. I know it."

The men sat in silence a few moments.

Peter cleared his throat. "There's talk that the British lost most of their officers in the battle."

"It's true," Salem said.

"Have you heard what the British plan to do next?" Peter asked.

Salem shook his head. "They're busy burying their dead in Boston." He looked over at Tobias. "What are your plans, son?"

Tobias stared at the glowing coals of the fire. The memory of the horrible battle flooded his thoughts. His heart felt heavy at the loss of Davy. He took a deep breath. "I'm heading to Boston."

"Boston?" Salem asked in surprise.

Tobias nodded. "I have friends there who need a drummer. They're making secret plans to organize a company to protect Boston and help drive out the British."

"Is this true?" Salem questioned.

Peter nodded. "A man by the name of Middleton has already started gathering volunteers. Word came in this morning."

"George Middleton said I could join his company as a drummer," Tobias said eagerly. "He's a friend of my uncle."

"I see," Salem said.

Caw! Caw! Caw! With a sudden flurry of black feathers, a crow flew down into the circle of men and landed in front of Tobias. He dropped a shiny coin on the ground.

"Davy!" Tobias cried, waves of sudden happiness washing over him. "Where have you been?" Tobias held out his arm and Davy hopped up to perch on his wrist. Oh, it felt good to know Davy was all right!

Peter reached out and picked up the coin. "A shilling! Now that's a true friend for you."

Tobias threw back his head and laughed.

Caw! Caw! Davy hopped up and down on Tobias's wrist.

"Now just what do you plan to do with a shilling?" Peter asked, handing it out to Tobias.

Tobias took the shilling. He grinned. "I'll use it to buy a new drumhead, of course!"

The History Behind the Story

PRIMARY AND SECONDARY SOURCES
WHICH TIE IN WITH THE STORY

The History Behind the Story

T he novel you just read, *A Dangerous Search,* by Nancy I. Sanders, is historical fiction. The author based the story upon actual people and events that occurred during the American Revolution. Many of the events in the story actually happened, such as the Siege of Boston and the Battle of Bunker Hill. Other events and situations are fictitious, such as a character named Tobias Gardner who tried to find his uncle and ended up joining the war as a drummer.

Most of the main characters Tobias met in the story actually took part in the Revolutionary War such as Lemuel Haynes and Salem Poor. More than 5,000 African American Patriots fought for the freedom of their country during this era, even though it would take another hundred years and another war to finally bring slavery to end. Some were offered their freedom to join the fight, but others volunteered. Willing to lay down their lives for liberties that they were often denied because of their race, these brave heroes will not be forgotten. Look at the primary source documents on the following pages to learn more about who some of these Patriots really were.

A primary source document is a written or verbal record of an event by people who were actually there when it happened. Even though the American Revolution took place more than 200 years ago, documents, maps, paintings, and songs from this time period can still be found today in libraries, museums, and private collections.

Peter Salem
(1750?-1816)

Peter Salem was one of the colonial militia who participated in the American Revolution from the very first day of fighting. He fought against the British troops at Concord and then fought again at the Battle of Bunker Hill. Some eyewitnesses to the battle claimed that Peter Salem was the man who shot and killed Major Pitcairn when the Redcoats attempted to storm into the redoubt, or fort, the Patriot troops had quickly constructed overnight.

When war broke out, Peter Salem was a slave. Yet he was given his freedom so he could fight for the freedom and liberties of America from England. He bravely served until the end of the war, when he returned home to Framingham, Massachusetts.

Peter Salem shooting British Major John Pitcairn in the Battle of Bunker Hill. (Negro History Association)

Prince Easterbrooks
(Also known as Estabrook)
(b.?-d.?)

When the Continental Congress called for groups of Minutemen to organize who would be ready to defend their country against British troops at a minute's notice, Prince Easterbrooks heard the cry. He enlisted and joined Captain John Parker's company at Lexington. Not many details are known about Easterbrooks' life, but his courage in the defense of liberty was immortalized through history when his name appeared in a broadside, or printed report, listing those who were killed or wounded at Concord. Prince Easterbrooks was listed among the wounded from Lexington.

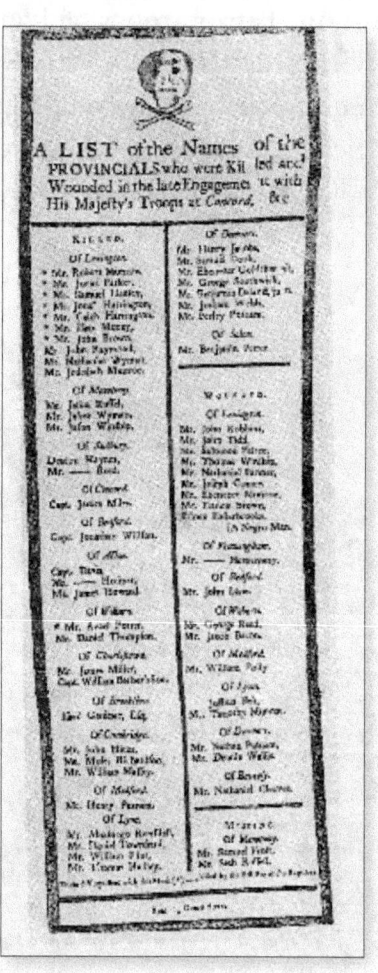

"A List of the Names of the Provincials who were Killed and Wounded in the late Engagement with His Majesty's Troops at Concord, &c."

Massachusetts Historical Society, broadside, undated The name of "Prince Easterbrooks, (A Negro Man)" is listed under the "Wounded of Lexington."

88

Barzillai Lew
(1743-1793?)

Born into a musical family of free blacks, Barzillai Lew enlisted as a fifer and drummer in the Twenty-Seventh Massachusetts Regiment shortly after the Battle of Lexington. He was remembered as inspiring the Patriot troops to be courageous during the Battle of Bunker Hill by playing "Yankee Doodle" on his fife. The powder horn he used during this famous battle can be found in the collections of the DuSable Museum of African American History in Chicago. Following in his footsteps, future generations of Lew's descendants continued to serve proudly in the United States military through the Civil War and on up to today.

Long thought to be of Barzillai Lew, this painting may actually be of his son, Barzillai Lew, Jr. (Diplomatic Reception Room, US Department of State, Washington, D.C.)

Lemuel Haynes
(1753-1833)

From the very beginning, Lemuel Haynes faced many challenges in his life, yet through determination, courage, and faith he accomplished amazing achievements. Haynes never knew his father, who was from Africa. His white mother abandoned him at birth. As an infant, he became an indentured servant to a white family in Granville, Massachusetts, until he reached the age of 21. During his youth, he attended a local school. Eager to learn, he continued studying on his own at home in the evenings by firelight.

When his term of indenture was over, Haynes enlisted as a Minuteman. After the outbreak of fighting at Lexington, he marched with his company of militia to join the Siege of Boston. With the fire of liberty burning in his heart, he wrote a lengthy poem about the skirmish on Lexington Green, acknowledging the deep significance of this battle. The words of his poem convey a strong sense of emotion about how the British soldiers attacked and killed the Patriots, or "Sons of Freedom," on that fateful day. He expresses how men would rather die fighting for their freedom than live as a slave to tyranny.

After the American Revolution, Haynes returned home to Granville where he married and had ten children. He studied Latin and Greek, and was ordained as a minister. During his long preaching career, he pastured white congregations in New England and New York. A man of letters, he continued to write other sermons and papers including a manuscript called "Liberty Further Extended." In this he boldly claims that the same liberties fought for during the Revolutionary War should be extended to those suffering in slavery. Because of his fame and important influence, Middlebury College awarded him an honorary master's degree, making Haynes the first African American to receive such an honor.

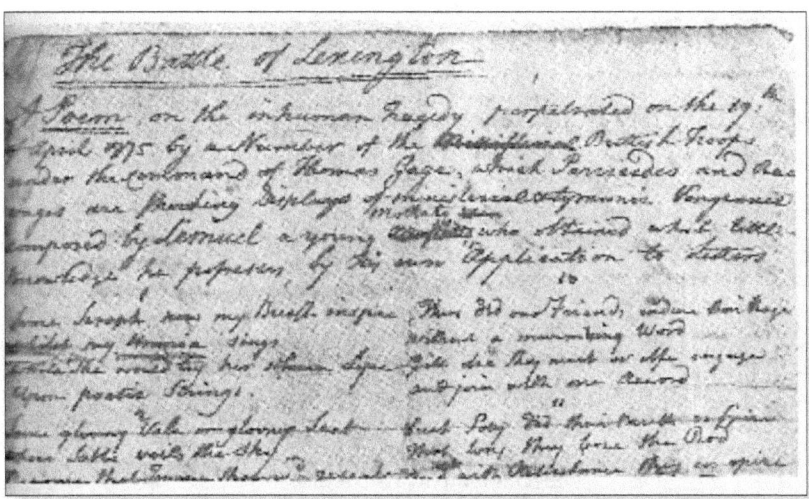

Excerpt from "The Battle of Lexington" by Lemuel Haynes (Houghton Library, Harvard University)

The Battle of Lexington
BY LEMUEL HAYNES

1

Some Seraph now my Breast inspire
whilst my Urania sings
while She would try her solemn Lyre
Upon poetic Strings.

2

Some gloomy Vale or gloomy Seat
where Sable veils the sky
Become that Tongue that wd repeat
The dreadfull Tragedy

3

The Nineteenth Day of April last
We ever shall retain
As monumental of the past
most bloody shocking Scene

4

Then Tyrants fill'd wth horrid Rage
A fatal Journey went
& Unmolested to engage
And slay the innocent

5

Then did we see old Bonner rise
And, borrowing Spite from Hell
They stride along with magic Eyes
where Sons of Freedom dwell

6

At Lexington they did appear
Array'd in hostile Form
And tho our Friends were peacefull there
Yet on them fell the Storm

7

Eight most unhappy Victims fell
Into the Arms of Death
unpitied by those Tribes of Hell
who curs'd them wth their Breath

8

The Savage Band still march along
For Concord they were bound
While Oaths & Curses from their Tongue
Accent with hellish Sound

9

To prosecute their fell Desire
At Concord they unite
Two Sons of Freedom there expire
By their tyrannic Spite

10

Thus did our Friends endure their Rage
without a murm'ring Word
Till die they must or else engage
and join with one Accord

11

Such Pity did their Breath inspire
That long they bore the Rod
And with Reluctance they conspire
to shed the human Blood

12

But Pity could no longer sway
Tho' 't is a pow'rfull Band
For Liberty now bleeding lay
And calld them to withstand

13

The awfull Conflict now begun
To rage with furious Pride
And Blood in great Effusion run
From many a wounded Side

14

For Liberty, each Freeman Strives
As it's a Gift of God
And for it willing yield their Lives
And Seal it with their Blood

15

Thrice happy they who thus resign
Into the peacefull Grave
Much better there, in Death Confin'd
Than a Surviving Slave

16

This Motto may adorn their Tombs,
(Let tyrants come and view)
"We rather seek these silent Rooms
"Than live as Slaves to You

17

Now let us view our Foes awhile
who thus for Blood did thirst
See: stately Buildings fall a Spoil
To their unstoick Lust

18

Many whom Sickness did compel
To seek some Safe Retreat
Were dragged from their sheltering Cell
And mangled in the Street

19

Nor were our aged Gransires free
From their vindictive Pow'r
On yonder Ground lo: there you see
Them weltering in their Gore

20

Mothers w ith helpless Infants strive
T' avoid the tragic Sight
All fearfull wether yet alive
Remain'd their Soul's delight

21

Such awefull Scenes have not had Vent
Since Phillip's War begun
Nay sure a Phillip would relent
And such vile Deeds would shun

22

But Stop and see the Pow'r of God
Who lifts his Banner high
Jehovah now extends his Rod
And makes our Foes to fly

23

Altho our Numbers were but few
And they a Num'rous Throng
Yet we their Armies do pursue
And drive their Hosts along

24

One Son of Freedom could annoy
A Thousand Tyrant Fiends
And their despotick Tribe destroy
And chace them to their Dens

25

Thus did the Sons of Brittain's King
Receive a sore Disgrace
Whilst Sons of Freedom join to sing
The Vict'ry they Imbrace

26

Oh! Brittain how are thou become
Infamous in our Eye
Nearly allied to antient Rome
That Seat of Popery

27

Our Fathers, tho a feeble Band
Did leave their native Place
Exiled to a desert Land
This howling Wilderness

28

A Num'rous Train of savage Brood
Did then attack them round
But still they trusted in their God
Who did their Foes confound

29

Our Fathers Blood did freely flow
To buy our Freedom here
Nor will we let our freedom go
The Price was much too dear

30

Freedom & Life, O precious Sounds
yet Freedome does excell
and we will bleed upon the ground
or keep our Freedom still

31

But oh! How can we draw the Sword
Against our native kin
Nature recoils as such a Word
And fain wd quit the Scene

32

We feel compassion in our Hearts
That captivating Thing
Nor shall Compassion once depart
While Life retains her String

33

Oh England let thy Fury cease
At this convulsive Hour
Consult those Things that make for Peace
Nor foster haughty Power

34

Let Brittain's king call home his Band
Of Soldiers arm'd to fight
To see a Tyrant in our Land
Is not a pleasing Sight

35

Allegiance to our King we own
And will due Homage pay
As does become his royal Throne
Yet in a legal Way

36

Oh Earth prepare for solemn Things
Behold an angry God
Beware to meet the King of Kings
Arm'd with an awefull Rod

37

Sin is the Cause of all our Woe
That sweet deluding ill
And till we let this darling go
There's greater Trouble still

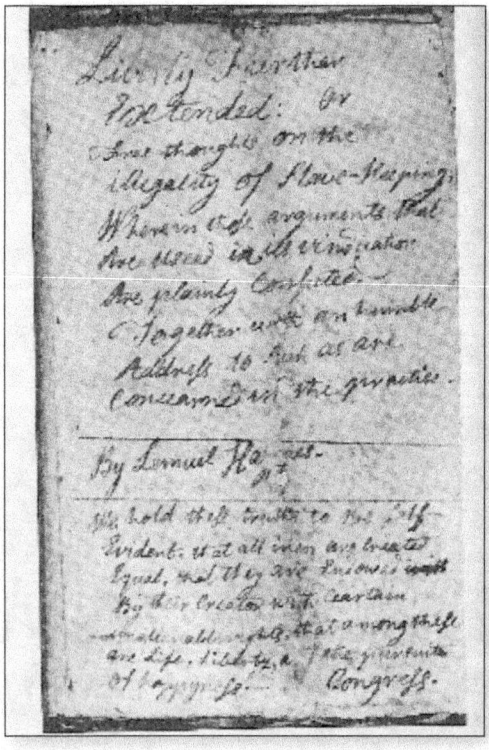

Excerpt from "Liberty Further Extended: or some thoughts on the illegality of slave-keeping" (Houghton Library, Harvard University)

Prince Hall
(1735?-1807)

During the American Revolution and the years after the war, Prince Hall was the most important African American leader in Boston. He organized and led Boston's black community in politics, anti-slavery issues, and the pursuit of equal rights.

Once a slave himself, Hall was eventually given his freedom. By the time war broke out, Hall owned and operated a successful leather working shop in Boston called the Golden Fleece. A bill of sale still exists today from Prince Hall to the Boston Regiment of Artillery concerning the sale of five leather drumheads.

Shortly before the fighting took place on Lexington Green, Hall took steps to form the first black Masonic lodge. At a time when there were no formal organizations to help African Americans, this was a monumental step. Hall had originally asked to become a member of Boston's Masonic lodge of Freemasons, but was turned away. Along with fourteen other free African Americans from Boston, Hall then approached a British army lodge of Freemasons, where they were given membership. African Lodge No. 459 was eventually formed, with Prince Hall as master.

Because of his outstanding leadership, outspoken protests against slavery, and tireless efforts for equal education and opportunity, Prince Hall influenced the Massachusetts government to bring an end to slavery in that state. He was also instrumental in helping bring an end to the trans-Atlantic slave trade, shortly after his death.

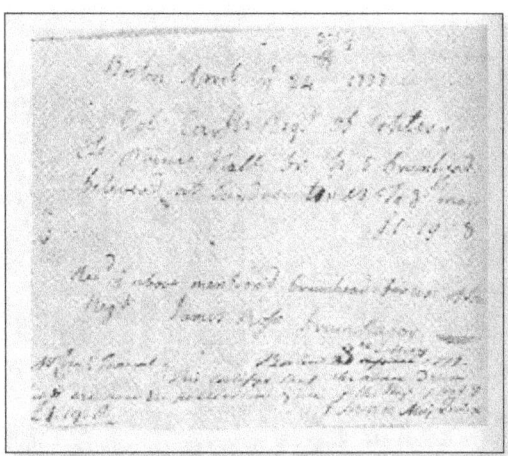

Bill of sale for drumheads from Prince Hall to Boston Regiment of Artillery, April 24, 1777 (Massachusetts Archives)

George Middleton
(1735-1815)

Close friends, George Middleton and Prince Hall worked together as leaders of the African American community in Boston. Not much is known for sure about Middleton's participation in the American Revolution because no official military records have been found. However, accounts are given of Colonel Middleton being presented with a silk flag by John Hancock in honor of the brave service he gave by leading an all-black unit from Boston called the Bucks of America. Known for his excellent horsemanship, Middleton also played the violin.

After the war, historical records indicate that Middleton spent the rest of his life fighting for the end of slavery, equal rights, and equal education opportunities for African American children in Boston. His house, one of the oldest original buildings from the Revolutionary Era still standing in Boston today, was often used as a place for important political gatherings. Middleton was one of the leading members of the Prince Hall Masons, becoming its third Grand Master after the death of Prince Hall. Together with Hall and other freemen of Boston, Middleton organized the African Benevolent Society, a group dedicated to helping the poor and improving the quality of life for the black citizens of Boston.

Badge of Bucks of America, Medallion, 1776-1780
Massachusetts Historical Society

The Bucks of America, silk flag,
40" x 62" 1776-1780
Presented by John Hancock to
George Middleton
Massachusetts Historical Society

Salem Poor
(1747?-1802?)

Of all the soldiers who fought at the Battle of Bunker Hill (also known as the Battle of Charlestown), only one was singled out to honor for his brave spirit and courageous actions. Even though we don't know the details, Salem Poor was truly the hero of the day. William Prescott and thirteen other officers filed a petition asking for Salem Poor to be rewarded for fighting like an experienced soldier with distinguished character during the battle.

Born into slavery, Salem Poor worked hard to save enough money to purchase his freedom. When war broke out in Lexington, he enlisted as a member of the Fifth Massachusetts Regiment. Eager to defend the liberty he prized so highly, he was part of the militia who worked all night building the fort on Bunker's Hill. Something must have happened in the fort during the terrible battle that followed which proved Poor was a brave hero, but records don't provide the details. We do know, however, that he is credited with having shot British officer James Abercrombie as he climbed over the fort wall, waving his arms in triumph.

After the Battle of Bunker Hill, Salem Poor continued to fight for his country. He suffered through the terrible winter at Valley Forge and served with the Continental Army until the end of the war.

The subscribers begg leave, to Report to your Honorable House (which wee do in justice to the caracter of so Brave a Man), that, under Our Own observation, Wee declare that a Negro Man, called Salem Poor, of Col. Fryes regiment, Capt. Ames company, in the late Battle at Charlestown, behaved like an Experienced officer, as well as an Excellent Soldier, to set forth Particulars of his conduct would be tedious. Wee would Only begg leave to say in the Person of this said Negro Centers a brave and gallant soldier. The Reward due to so great and Distinguisht a Caracter, Wee submit to the Congress.

The Petition for Salem Poor

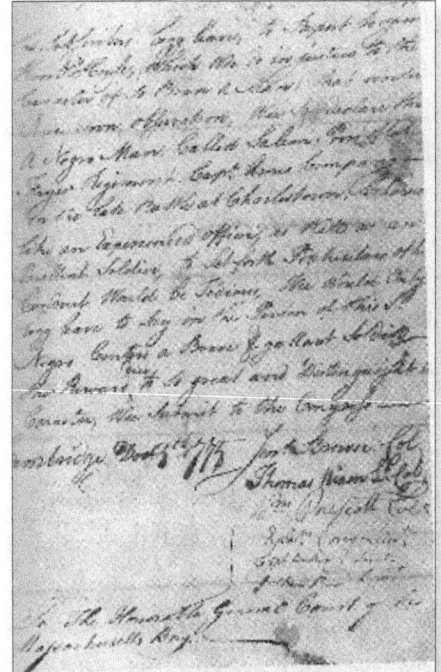

Petition to recognize bravery of Salem Poor at the Battle of Bunker Hill, December 5, 1775
(Massachusetts Archives)

Cambridge, Dec. 1775

Jona Brewer, Col.
Thomas Nixon Lt. Col
Wm. Prescott Col.
Ephm Corey Lieut
Joseph Baker Lieut
Joshua Reed Lieut

To the Honorable General Court of the Massachusetts Bay

Jonas Richardson Capt
Eliphalet Bodwell Left
Josiah Foster Lieut
Ebenr Varnum Lt
Wm Hudson Ballard Capt
William Smith Capn
John Martin
Lieut Richard Welsh

About the Author

Nancy I. Sanders is the bestselling and award-winning author of over 80 books, including several nonfiction books for children on African American history. These are *America's Black Founders* (www.AmericasBlackFounders.wordpress.com) the Award Winner in the Best Books 2010 Awards for children's nonfiction, *Frederick Douglass for Kids* (www.FrederickDouglass.wordpress.com) a 2012 Silver NAPPA Winner, and *A Kid's Guide to African American History* (www.AKidsGuide.wordpress.com). Her picture book, *D is for Drinking Gourd: An African American Alphabet* (www.DrinkingGourdAlphabet.wordpress.com) is winner of numerous awards including the 2008 IRA Teachers' Choice Award. Nancy also teams up with her husband, Jeff, a fourth grade elementary teacher, to write books for teachers to use in their classroom such *Readers Theatre for African American History*. Nancy and Jeff live in southern California with their two cats, Sandman and Pitterpat. Their two adult sons (Dan, and Ben with his delightful wife Christina) live nearby. To learn more about Nancy and her books, please visit her site at www.nancyisanders.com.

www.ingramcontent.com/pod-product-compliance
Lightning Source LLC
Chambersburg PA
CBHW071334130626
46556CB00004B/1891